Airship 27 Productions

AN AIRSHIP 27 PRODUCTION

Pulp Mythology

"Hercules the Conqueror" © 2018 Jamie L. Evans
"No Wrath Like a Nymph Scorned" © 2018 Joel Jenkins
"The City in the Clouds" © 2018 Barbara Doran
"Beowulf: The Schemes of Unferth" & "Procrustes" © 2018 Fred Adams Jr.

Published by Airship 27 Productions
www.airship27.com
www.airship27hangar.com

Interior illustrations ©2018 Clayton Hinkle
Cover illustration © 2018 Zachary Brunner

Editor: Ron Fortier
Associate Editor: Jaime Ramos
Marketing and Promotions Manager: Michael Vance
Production and design by Rob Davis.

ISBN-13: 978-1-946183-45-3
ISBN-10: 1-946183-45-8

Printed in the United States of America

10 9 8 7 6 5 4 3 2 1

Contents

Hercules the Conqueror

BY
JAMIE L. EVANS

The landscape was littered far and wide with bronze, hardened, dying men that have fallen in a massive battle. They lay across two hundred yards of blood-drenched fields. Above the painful groaning, the shouts of others could be heard as the black vultures plucked at their flesh. Insects wormed into open wounds, everywhere smelled of damp mildew and nauseating rotting flesh. Contorted, scarred, blacken bodies of the enemy also lie in the fields. Hercules peered down from a nearby hillside as the picture he encountered produced tears to his eyes.

"Zeus, why has this happened? Why?"

Hercules abruptly wakens, sitting up quickly in his bed.

"Everything all right Hercules?" asked his wife, Megara.

Hercules nodded. "Just a nightmare."

"The same one?"

Hercules nodded again. "No matter. We have a big day today. We must get ready for our journey."

Hercules got up and quickly dressed. He hesitated for a moment and looked out his large window fronting the city. He took a deep breath. That was his last battle. Long after the Twelve Labors. He trained those men, but it was not enough. They died. He lived.

He slid his knife into his boot and took his sword and slid it silently in its sheath. He looked up and half smiled.

"You ready?" He said to Megara as she reentered the room.

"I am, and I am excited about this trip. It has been too long since we traveled together."

"Agreed. This should be an easy journey, but be on alert."

"Always," smiled Megara as she sheathed her dagger.

While they had an early start to the day, night soon arrived. As Hercules built a fire, Megara took care of their horses and then cooked a simple meal. They could hear numerous wild beasts bellowing in the shadows of darkness. As the night turned pitch black with barely any stars to light the sky on such a clouded murky night, Hercules remained on guard while Megara slept. He finally fell asleep as well with his hand on his sword and one eye on the fire.

Suddenly there came a loud scream, shut off in mid-note. Hercules sprung up with his sword ready. Megara woke up as well as she grabbed her dagger.

"What was that Hercules?"

Hercules said nothing as he scanned the darkness intently, ready to catch the slightest of sounds. Hercules finally spoke.

"Grab some fire. Hand me one as well."

Megara picked up two large sticks and wrapped some anointed cloth around them, lit them and handed one to Hercules. Grabbing the horses, Hercules and Megara moved away from their camp. Hercules studied the ground carefully and noticed human tracks in the sand, not of a man, but of a woman. He pointed them out to Megara as she nodded in agreement. As daylight began to peer through the thick morning haze, fire was no longer needed, so Hercules tossed his torch aside. He covertly followed the easily identifiable tracks as they headed into a slot canyon for a mile before turning and following a stream that emerged from a crack in the canyon wall. They continued a hundred yards up the stream. Hercules stopped. He smelled the air and proceeded slowly past a projecting rock. Discreetly peering around the large rock, halfway up the hillside, he discovered two creatures sitting on the ledge. They were womanlike, yet hardly women. Most would never visualize a creature so strangely beautiful. They were stunning to view while the morning dew glistened on their naked skin as they basked in the early morning sunrise. These strange creatures had the facial features of celestial Goddesses, while their scalps crawled with massive snakes. As they stretched, Hercules could see the position of their bodies as their legs slouched from the torso sloping forward from the hips and their heads bent toward the ground. Their arms were long, making it appear almost as though they were crawling on all fours. Their hands were large and the fingers were razor sharp claws.

"Gorgons," Hercules identified. "Haven't seen their type in ages!"

He decided to confront them. He didn't want any innocent traveler to meet these two. And by the sound they had heard earlier, someone had already done so. Hercules jumped down with his sword drawn as the closer Gorgon turned and released a guttural scream. As Hercules' sword cleaved into the Gorgon's shoulder, it howled in excruciating pain. Blood spurted upward from its shoulder and its mouth, as it fell to its knees. Blood squirted out from its neck. Hercules retrieved his sword stuck in the creature's shoulder and maneuvered it around his waist. With the sword now in his left hand, he swung it as the second Gorgon closed in for an attack. His sword struck the Gorgon in the neck, cleaning dissecting the head, causing it to fly through the air, with spurting blood further projecting the head upwards. As it landed behind Hercules with a small thud, he quickly looked around and found no other Gorgons present. He thought for a moment that there may have been two more. He cleaned off his sword and quickly re-sheathed. Megara came out of the brush.

"So much for that easy trip to Panemorfi,"she smiled.

Hercules returned the smile.

"We have a day more to journey. To save time I've decided we should go through the Gigantas woodlands. We must not be late to meet the boat to Panemorfi. So we'll leave at daybreak."

Megara nodded in approval.

✝✝✝

Hercules and Megara journeyed well into the night. The moon was high up in the night sky, shining its yellow glow on them, helping to light their way. They finally made it to the end of the valley, right at the border of the Gigantas woodlands. The first tree of the forest was so vast that Hercules and Megara's horses looked like ants.

"Wow," said Megara as she looked up at the giant tree. "I see why they named this place Gigantas."

"Yes," agreed Hercules, "it is most impressive, but we must be cautious. The trees aren't the only things in Gigantas woodland that grow to such massive proportions. Too many giant beasts call this forest home; we would be little more than a nice little snack."

"It's pretty dark in there," Megara pointed out.

"And it's too dangerous to go in during the night. We should camp here," Hercules decided. "We can start again at first light."

"Fine by me," said Megara as she dismounted. "My backside is killing me."

"We need to get a fire going quickly."

"I'll go collect the firewood," Megara said.

"Be careful remember strange beast roam these woods."

"Don't worry and don't forget it's your turn to cook us a meal," Megara reminded him as she walked away.

Hercules had put up their tent by the time Megara finally came back with firewood. Hercules took several logs and branches, piling the smaller twigs loosely while stacking the larger logs on top, to build a fire in the pit that he had made. He then pulled out a stone along with a piece of steel, striking them against each other, as they created sparks, starting a massive fire.

"Hercules," Megara said as loudly as she dared, "I don't think we're alone."

Hercules leaped to his feet as he drew his sword. He saw several sets of eyes in the darkness, glowing yellow in the firelight. Hercules pulled Megara close to him, standing shoulder to shoulder facing outwards around the fire. The eyes were all around them, surrounding them. Then there was movement from one of the observers as it edged into the light. It's was a massively large wolf, the size of a horse. Then another wolf stepped out of the shadows with three more following. Soon they were surrounded by these gigantic wolves, circling them like sharks, snarling while emitting low guttural growls.

"Hercules, let me," offered Megara.

The largest wolf from the pack cautiously approached Megara. She bravely extended her hand as the carefully sniffed, picking up her scent. Suddenly, its ears perked up as it began wagging its tail as it knocked the dark skinned woman onto her back and began licking her face. Almost immediately, the other wolves in the pack began to jump about like a bunch of playful pups. Megara laughed as she scratched the wolf behind the ear. She whispered in the ear of the great wolf and off it went through the forest.

"Megara how did you do that?" Hercules asked incredulously.

"Hercules you know I speak to animals."

"Yes, in our village. But they are just dogs and horses. This is most impressive."

Megara laughed. "I asked him to find us food."

"Will they return?" Hercules inquired.

"If they can find food." says Megara,

A few hours after they had left, the wolf pack returned with dinner.

Three of the wolves each had a single rabbit in its mouth which they happily dropped at Megara's feet. Like the woodlands and all that inhabits it, the rabbits were not of normal size, each was about the scale of a full grown sheep. Hercules took one, hauling it over to the tent, where he began skinning and cleaning it. As he did this, Megara turned to the wolves, which looked at her patiently.

"We thank you, my friends," she said. "But I'm afraid we can't possibly eat all three rabbits. We will take the one and you may have the rest."

The wolves let out a series of barks in gratitude. That night Hercules and Megara enjoyed a hearty meal. Even with Hercules' giant appetite, just one of those rabbits was enough to satiate his hunger. The wolf pack stayed around the camp as they slept as not many creatures would willingly attack a pack of giant wolves. When they woke the following morning, the wolves were gone.

†††

Hercules and Megara continued traveling deeper into the woods, trying to keep to a trail that was long ago forgotten. Hercules held up his right hand and Megara stopped. Hercules listened carefully. He looked back to Megara and pointed to his left and whispered.

"Giants."

There in the distance was an enormous giant, old and gray with a beard that came down to his stomach while next to him sat a younger giant with a nasty scar splayed across his forehead. The younger giant was poking at their fire with a short stick. The older giant placed a hand on his stomach as it growled in protest.

"I hungry," stated Greybeard, "Why you not put meat on that stick?"

"Meat all run away, Greybeard," responded the younger giant. "We not catch any for days."

"But I hungry," Greybeard complained.

"Me hungry too," replied his companion.

"We not be hungry if you catch meat," argued Greybeard.

"We no catch meat 'cause there no meat to catch" shouted the youngster.

"I know where you can find meat," countered a mysteriously feminine voice.

"Who say that?" shouted Greybeard.

"I not say nothing," said the surprised youngster.

"I did," replied the voice again.

Out into the clearing, strolled two Gorgons wearing no clothing at all. The older giant fell over a giant tree stump as they drew closer.

"Human are near and you may have human meat," reported the first Gorgon.

"Humans. Riding horses," added the second one.

"Me like human meat," declared Greybeard.

"Horse meat good, human meat dangerous. They carry sharp things," warned the youngster.

Greybeard picked up a huge log, "We carry big crushies!"

"Greybeard smart," the youth acknowledged. "He know humans. He try eat them before."

As the Gorgons stared intimately into the giants in the eyes, each summoned their innate magic, causing their eyes to glow red. The eyes of the giants responded with a glow of red as well. The giants hoisted boulders and a tree log and started heading out to look for the humans.

"Zeus!" cried Hercules.

"Meat!" shouted Greybeard as he swung his gigantic club at Hercules, narrowly missing the demigod.

"Zeus!" shouted Hercules again as he drew his blade.

"Scatter!" cried Megara as she started her horse away from the giants.

"Agreed!" Hercules he pointed his sword at the younger giant.

"Look at the young giant!"

"What about him?" asks Megara as her husband ducked under a flying boulder.

"He looks just like Zeus!" hollered the Hercules.

"By the gods!" exclaimed Megara. "You're right! But really, who...?"

The older giant swung his club at Megara, missing her by inches.

"Who cares what they look like?" shouted Megara. "Just kill them before they kill us!"

"Maybe your wolf friends might show up!" Hercules yelled.

"That would be nice!"

Hercules leapt off of his horse and dove behind a large tree, just as Zeus' doppelganger heaved a large boulder, cracking it against the trunk of the tree, barely missing Hercules. Hercules stepped out, picking up a giant stone, hurled it at the giant. It struck the giant, but was so small that it didn't affect him. Greybeard charged at Hercules with his giant club. Hercules dashed away just in time, letting the club practically knock over the tree he had been hiding behind. Megara fired an arrow from her bow at the old giant. The arrow hit the flesh of the old giant, but caused no damage. Hercules ran by, slicing the club in two with his sword.

"Megara!" He called out. "Go for the eyes! It's our only chance!"

"I'm ready when you are," replied Megara.

"NOW!"

Megara blasted Greybeard in the face with her arrows, each of them focusing on a different eye. As their arrows easily found their targets, Greybeard roared in agony, clutching his injured eyes as he staggered backward, tripping over a fallen tree, falling hard onto his back. Hercules picked up one of the giants' discarded boulders and hurled it at the younger giant. The large rock hit the youthful giant in the face. He was still for a moment then rocked back and forth until he fell face down to the ground causing it to tremble.

Quickly escaping before the Gorgons could continue the attack, Hercules and Megara jumped on their horses and swiftly rode off. Hercules pointed straight ahead towards a ray of light breaking through the thick forest. Megara took a deep breath, smelling the ocean nearby. Both rode on through the forest finally arriving at a sandy beach.

"It's beautiful," exclaimed Megara.

"It is, and look!" Hercules pointed to his left, on the horizon, their ship lazily rocked about in the sea.

"We made it on time," Megara laughed happily.

They could see Hercules companion, Iolaus waving to them from the bow.

☦☦☦

After boarding themselves and the horses on the ship, Hercules and Megara spent a few minutes relating their recent adventures with Iolaus, a handsome man with corn yellow hair. Then both rested comfortably as the ship prepared to get underway. An unexpected delay occurred as a strange thick, heavy fog rolled in, the kind that is felt deep in the lungs, making it hard to breathe. Hercules was not happy with this fog as it seemed unnatural like some mystic power had control of it. He kept this thought to himself, not wanting to worry Megara. The ship finally left dock slowly, creeping out to the large vast ocean. To ease the crew and Megara, Hercules decided to tell a tale of one of his twelve adventures. A crew member spoke out.

"Hercules we have heard the stories of your Twelve Labors many times. Let's hear one of your new adventures!"

The crew of the ship cheered as Megara nodded in approval. Hercules thought for a moment and then decided to tell them a sea adventure. He twisted around and leaned back against the mast of the ship.

"I have one for you, a sea adventure I had many years ago against the Satyr."

"Who?" someone yelled.

"The Satyr," Hercules spoke louder. "Their island is near here and I recommend we do not sail too close. It was many years ago. After a storm, my crew and I found ourselves washed up, stranded on a strange island inhabited by these Satyrs."

"What sort of people are they?" yelled a crew member.

"They were born from the evil Typhon, half man, half goat. While some tribes on other lands are very friendly, these were bred to be warriors."

"Could they fight?"

"Yes," Hercules said. "But not well. They had heart, but they were no match for my men and me. Yet they were many, and the battle was long. Most died that day."

Megara looked up and knew he was talking about his last brutal battle. The one that he has nightmares about every night. Hercules leaned forward, picked up a jug of wine and took a big drink. He wiped his mouth reflectively.

"We found out that there was hidden treasure on the island that they guarded, but we were in exhausted from the extensive battle and in a hurry and could not press them anymore for answers. I still think back to that island and the treasures it might still have. I would love to go back and take revenge for the men we lost."

Hercules rose, walking to the steps of the ship. Upon climbing to the top of the forecastle, he viewed the ship's surroundings. There was a slight wind coming from land. He was hopeful that the fog would lift soon. Yet the wind shifted and Hercules knew that this was no natural wind. This was mystic.

"Tell us more," a crew member shouted towards Hercules.

Hercules said nothing. He was still looking out to the vast ocean. Waiting. Hercules was correct when he said that the Satyr Island was near. Yet with the wind and the fog he did not know how near!

Suddenly, disguised by the thick fog, the armed Satyr emerged and began swarming over the ship. They were unwashed filthy creatures.

"Tell us more!"

Hercules cried out a warning. "They are here! Ready yourselves for battle!"

A Satyr jumped in front of Hercules. He struck out, his fist finding its left jaw sending the Satyr overboard. The sailors were used to fighting in close and ever ready to defend the ship. Hercules looked for Megara and saw her knife a Satyr in the throat. Then she kicked its body over the side. Hercules was proud of his mate's fighting prowess. She was better than most men he knew. He was busy himself, holding a Satyr in each hand and cracking their heads together. In the stern, Hercules best friend Iolaus, was making short work of three Satyr. The encounter did not last long for which Hercules was grateful. With the way the Satyr swung their swords, they might have knocked a few holes in the hull. Hercules breathed easier when the last of them went down.

"Now," he said. "Maybe we can question to one of them."

Hercules tried to recall the language of the Satyr as he hauled a large Satyr to his feet.

"Look here. Can you understand me?"

Then the sun came up, and the Satyr got a look at the man who held him.

"I understand you." His words came through chattering teeth.

"Good. Don't be afraid. We mean no harm."

As Hercules questioned the Satyr, he studied it carefully. The Satyr explained of needing more sacrifices for the priests and that the girl was almost ready.

"What kind of priests?" Hercules inquired.

"The Silenus," it whispered.

"Is that what they are called? How far to this land?"

The Satyr was scared, shaking his head negatively in response. Some of his friends were coming around. They were all turning pale at the demigod's line of questioning. It was obvious to Hercules that there wasn't going to be any further answers from these survivors.

"Tell him he'll drown in the ocean unless he talks," Iolaus suggested.

Hercules hesitated. Fighting was one thing, torture was another. It was all right to cut a man to pieces as long as he had a chance to do the same to you. Maybe threats would do the trick. He told the Satyr what the crew member had suggested, and the man licked his lips. The rest of the Satyr were in a panic, babbling among themselves. Hercules understood enough of what they were saying as they all pointed to the sun. *What the devil?* He thought. Were the Silenus some sort of Sun Gods? No, that wasn't it either.

From what he had heard, they had some type of power that came from the sun, that could turn a man to cinders. To speak too much about them would mean death.

"Talk you live, don't talk you go for a swim," Hercules pointed to the water.

He narrowed his eyes, making them as cruel as he could. He drew the sword from his sheath, running his finger along the extremely sharp edge. His sword glinted in the sunlight, hovering at the man's throat.

"I will tell you all I know," the Satyr said resignedly.

Hercules looked over to Megara. "We are making a stop before we reach Panemorfi."

Megara nodded.

†††

They found an inlet that was a perfect hiding place for the ship. There were enough branches hanging to screen it from distant eyes. Yet Hercules had the feeling that they were being watched. He swung around suddenly, seeing nothing but the gently waving branches. A harmless scene, the rushing waters of the inlet and the serenity of the woods, and yet he felt evil was near. Hercules did not trust the Satyr, but it looked as their captive had directed them honestly. Up the coast and down a small channel, they had sailed around the southern cape then transitioned westward 'til they found the right island and its channel. From here forward, they would travel on land. Somewhere ahead was an embankment and there Hercules would find what he was looking for.

"I have a feeling," Iolaus muttered as they marched along.

He was a foot shorter than Hercules, but with an expansive chest that threatened to burst through his breastplate. His arms were just as big as Hercules.

"So have I," Hercules admitted. "In my bones."

Out of the north came a scent like an opened grave. They walked stealthily through the forest with their hands on their swords. The twilight was quite long on this island which brought shadows that could deceive any man. A strange land was this, where Spring came early and where the air was soft. Hercules looked over to Megara, sensing her fear. He understood for he was frightened as well. Yet for some reason he was compelled to go to this island. He thought perhaps the Gods had wished him to go, but was not sure. Swords were worthless here, the Satyr had said. A man's strength meant nothing. The Satyr claimed all they would find at the end of their journey was death. A voice whispered in Hercules's mind that the Satyr might be right. But there was another voice, a voice that had grown stronger as he sailed southward. This was a voice that came from the heavens.

"I hear something," Megara whispered. "I hear something inside my head."

Hercules turned surprised. "You hear it too?"

The others nodded in agreement, confirming that they all heard it as well. They stared at each other in the gathering dusk. Magic was at play, but Hercules believed it was a sinister magic. Night had fallen with the last hint of dusk disappearing over the peak, quickly engulfing them into darkness. On a far off peak, a fire burst upward. Flames of yellow and blue rose tall. Was it a beacon to lure them to their doom? They paused in a grove, surrounded within a circle of stones. It was time to rest as weariness crept over them. Hercules studied the stones noticing that they were abnormal, somehow unnatural. They had been placed there! He knew then how strong the dark forces were. His inner voice warned him of the danger that lurked in this circle of stones. Yet the power was so strong, Hercules felt lethargic. He saw the men begin to stagger.

Summoning up his last reserve of strength, he positioned his foot against one of the stones and kicked it away, causing it to tumble down the hillside. The circle was broken along with its spell. Hercules physically shook himself to remove the lethargy that clung to him. He had learned one thing, to stay outside stone circles.

Hercules and his continued on to a small cliff allowing them to view the flames they had spotted earlier. Now the fire was below them and they could hear the strange beings that surrounded it. Before the fire pit was a slab of white stone on which a figure was tied.

Hercules bade his companions to be quiet and leaning over the rock's edge, listened intently. A tall fellow stepped closer to the hot flames so that Hercules could see him clearer. His captive was a woman who appeared to be unconscious.

"The girl stirs," said the man Hercules deduced to be some kind of high priest.

His beard was black and thick, his skin white, with a circular scar on his forehead. Was it a battle scar or a mystic tattoo? The air was damp as the priest looked down upon the woman. In the light of the fire, her eyelids seemed to move. The cleric's fingers hovered at the hilt of a sacrificial knife.

"She stirs," another man whispered. "Tomorrow she will awaken. Let it be for the last time. As long as she lives, we are in danger."

"She can do nothing alone."

"But she is never alone. How many times has her beauty brought men to her aid?"

"We need them as well, for our sacrifices," the high-priest said. His eyes were bright beneath hooded lids.

"What about those who landed today?" suggested another of the group.

"They are somewhere nearby. We thought we had them, in one of our circles, but they broke away."

Hercules peered down intently attempted to count how many were present. His investigation was interrupted by footsteps echoing inside a nearby cave. A hooded priest came hurrying out of the cave and raced over to the high-priest. His fingers traced the sacred symbols in the night's damp air.

"Well?" the leader snapped. "What is it? News of the strangers?"

"We are having trouble following them. Their thoughts are shrouded. Something comes between them and us."

The high-priest's eyes darted back to the girl on the stone. He knew what it was that protected these strangers. Even in her sleep, the girl had power.

"Tomorrow, then," he announced loudly. "In the meantime, watch her. You two go and find our visitors."

Hercules looked over his shoulder to the crew, motioning for them to follow him. He moved swiftly and the others had all they could do to keep up with him. They quickly covered several miles going down a jungle path that led to the sacrificial altar below. It was Hercules' plan to attack the priest and his followers.

"We'll come at them straight ahead," Iolaus said, moving up to Hercules's side. "They'll never know what hit them."

✞✞✞

In the starlight, Hercules could see his outline with Iolaus' bulk next to him. Maybe the usual method of attack was best. Maybe Iolaus was right. Yet there was this knowledge that swords would not be enough. That meant mere strength did not matter. Disrupting his thoughts, Hercules caught the sound of voices. Out of the darkness ahead came a deep-throated, monotonous chant. They followed the eerie incantations through the trees coming upon a large clearing. Huge stones, too great for a man to move, formed a perfect circle. Towering thirty feet above the others were two monoliths standing a few feet apart and directly before them was the stone altar and the raging fire-pit behind it. Around the altar hooded shadows moved slowly, murmuring their endless chants. Hercules was tempted to strike immediately for they had the element of surprise on their side. But Hercules felt something was wrong. He held up his hand and motioned the crew to stop.

Megara was near him, whispering "The woman? Where is she?" His wife pointed to the altar and he saw only the ropes that had bound the female victim. What was going on here?

"Quiet," he whispered.

He continued to wait and was glad that he had. There was the faint flickering light of a torch that seemed to come out of the very ground beyond the circle of stones. It did come out of the ground. There was an opening of some sort, the mouth of another cave. As two figures emerged, he saw them clearly before the torch was extinguished. As he continued to secretly observe the pair, even in the dim starlight, Hercules saw one of the figures move away.

"Only one of them is guarding the opening," Megara stated the obvious.

"In that case, there must be something to guard. The woman must have been moved underground," he concluded.

"And perhaps the treasure in there!" Iolaus grinned.

"Listen," Hercules spoke softly. "I'm going to try to get inside."

"Alone?" Megara reacted.

"One is better than a dozen for this job. He seems to have pulled back into the mouth of the tunnel. If I can get him quickly, his friends may never notice he's gone."

"What about us?"

"You wait here. It's almost dawn. I should be back by then."

"And if you're not?"

"Then go back to the ship as fast as you can. There's no use trying if I can't get through. Don't ask me how I know that. I just do. That's an order. Understand? Trust me, I'll be all right."

Reluctantly his friends acquiesced. Hercules unbuckled his sword, and handed his shield to Megara. Next come off was the breastplate. When a man's greatest need was stealth, he didn't want any metal on him. A moment later he was off through the thin screen of trees, moving silently around the great circle of stones and fire pit. At every step, he felt the voice inside his head getting stronger. He knew he had to keep out of the circle. As he crept along, he arrived behind the slight rise in the earth that encompassed the opening of the tunnel.

Very slowly now, Hercules moved, feeling his way. He felt the rock beneath his fingers. Advancing a few more steps, the rock wall ended. He turned inward. Hugging the wall he inched forward. There was a shadow, darker than the rest. Lips moved in the darkness, forming soundless words. Hercules's hands reach out, finding a throat, quickly exerting enough pressure for the lips to abruptly stop moving. Hercules lifted the body, carrying it back away from the tunnel's entrance. He almost fell down the stone staircase that yawned suddenly at his feet.

When Hercules had recovered his poise, he went on, taking each step gingerly. As he headed down into a darkness the pungent smell of a dungeon mingling with even worse stench. The walls grew damp and clammy where he touched them. Slimy things scurried across the floor. The path Hercules was following twisted and turned. Suddenly a door appeared along the wall as Hercules fumbled in the darkness. He opened the door soundlessly. Beyond it was a faint and fitful light that led him onward toward its source, leading him directly into a extremely small restrictive room. Hercules knew it was the end of the search. Its bareness told him what he had already suspected. No typical treasures were to be found as these people did not believe in jeweled trappings. Yet in this very room, the true treasure was contained, the only thing that truly mattered, the girl. A black-robed figure with a broad back, wearing the folds of the dark priesthood, hid the sarcophagus from Hercules's view. The figure shifted uneasily, as though feeling eyes upon it as Hercules caught a glimpse of something beyond.

He cautiously stepped forward. Upon taking another step, his foot hit a rock, creating a faint noise, almost inaudible, but the high-priest man heard. He swiftly turned, unexpectedly seeing Hercules close the gap between them in a single leap. His left hand caught the priest's wrist, forcing the knife back. But the holy man was a tricky one, making it hard to hold him. He shifted, kicked out, causing Hercules to stumble. The knife was thrust near his face. Quickly Hercules' powerful fist struck the priest in the face killing him instantly. In an ornate casket, covered only in a thinly transparent white veil, lay a naked, breathtakingly beautiful woman, with raven black hair and full blood red lips. A thousand sleeps she had slept, and more. Older than the land from which Hercules had come, and yet she was younger than he.

"Wake up," Hercules shook her arm. Then, louder, "Wake up!"

Was she dead? He noticed she was breathing. He called to her again, trying to wake her. His voice was insistent, commanding. Very slowly, she opened her eyes. Blankly staring, she hovered on the brink of an eternal sleep. Hercules's will pulled her to life. The blankness went out of her eyes, replaced by a sudden gladness.

"You came. I knew you would come."

She struggled to sit up, blushing as she realized that only the veil covered her nudity. Hercules turned his back, bent and removed the black robe from the crumpled figure on the floor. Over his shoulder, he handed the robe to the girl. When he turned to her again, she was sitting up with a trace of color still in her cheeks.

"Where are they?" the woman named Calypso asked fearfully.

There was loathing in the glance she threw at the priest's body. "There are many more. Where are they?"

"Up above," Hercules told her. "This one and another were left to watch you."

"Good. They won't be coming back for any time soon now that hey are busy preparing for their sacrifices for the feast of Typhon." At that she shuddered.

Hercules spoke quickly. "What sort of men are they?"

"They are not men. They are Silenus. A long time ago they came out of the sea. They brought strange powers and a strange god who demanded human sacrifices. My people were driven out, killed. I am the only one left."

"But why did they save you?"

"As a hostage, at first. Later, because it pleased them to keep me as a symbol of the race they had vanquished. Every year I have awakened, they have used me as a mock sacrifice, then placing me to sleep again for another year."

"And today again?"

"For the last time. They have lost their power to act at a distance. They grow afraid that I may call someone they cannot defeat. Their power is great now on only this one day when the sun comes directly between the two stones they brought with them from their mother world."

She started suddenly, and Hercules stared at her.

"What is it?" he demanded.

"My people were driven out, killed. I am the only one left."

"I feel something. I feel danger."

There was no time to ask questions. Hercules knew she would not be wrong. This daughter of a lost people had a knowledge he could not fathom. He lifted her out of the sarcophagus and set her on her feet.

"We've got to get out of here. Once we reach my crew and set back for the coast, they'll never stop us."

They started running back along the corridor down which Hercules had come. Half way to the extim they heard the voices and the feet that came toward them from above. Hercules listened intently. There were too many. One or two he would have fought, maybe even a half-dozen. But this was the trample of many feet. They must have found the body at the head of the stairs. Hercules cursed his luck.

"We'll have to go back. Is there another way out?"

"No none. It was the burial place for the kings of my people before the Silenus came."

And it looked like it would be his burial place as well, Hercules thought. But he had to go back anyway. He couldn't take a chance on the girl being hurt in a fight in the dark. Besides, that fellow he had killed had a knife. It would be better than no weapon at all. The footsteps were closing in behind them as they ran. The girl was too slow. Hercules scooped her up and ran with her under his arm, but still was not swiftly enough. They had been overheard. He had barely enough time to swing Calypso behind the sarcophagus and out of immediate danger. He bent and tore the knife from the priest's loose grasp.

And then they were on him, a flood of black-robed figures. Blood spurted as the knife in Hercules's hand flashed. A man screamed, and then another as Hercules's fist made pulp of flesh and bone. His hands struck blows like a giant hammer. He made them pay dearly for every backward step he took. But they came on still. They were too many for him and they eventually forced him back until a cold wall stopped him. Then, by the sheer force of numbers, they overwhelmed him. He went down under a torrent of blows that drove everything from his mind but the thought that he had failed Calypso.

Daylight and Hercules's head ached as consciousness returned. He seemed to be a single aching bruise from head to foot. After awhile, he realized that Calypso lay beside him at the bottom of the stairs that led to the tunnel's mouth. The light came down strongly, too strongly. It was long after dawn. A stray thought flashed across Hercules's mind: his men would be well on their way to the ship: Yet there was no use castigating himself. Calypso would have died before they could have reached her if they had rushed in all together.

"I'm sorry," Hercules said and tried to turn toward Calypso.

Leather thongs bound him tightly, but he rocked back and forth until he tipped onto his side.

"Not as sorry as I," she said, her eyes soft on his face. "If I had not called, you would never have come."

"I am not afraid to die."

But he wasn't ready to die yet. He would not leave Megara. If he could only get a little play into the ropes that bound him! His muscles bulged with the strain as he threw all his strength into the effort. Then a scream filtered down and sent a shiver along his spine.

"The sacrifices have started," Calypso said. "It will not be long now. They will be coming for us soon."

"Can't...you...do anything?" Hercules asked as he continued to struggle against his restraints. "Can't you fight them with their own weapons?"

"Not while I am awake. When I sleep my soul is in communion with my people who have gone, and I draw strength from them. While the sun comes directly between the two great stones, the magic of the Silenus is at its most potent. And mine is waning."

†††

As her voice faded there came the scream again of a soul in mortal fear. The scream died quickly, merging into a rising paean from the Silenus. Then there was a patter of sandal-clad feet as the light from above was blocked by the figure of Diavolos, as yet another high priest. In Diavolos' hand, a great sacrificial knife dripped blood. Their god, Hestia would drink well this day, Hestia would be appeased. Behind Diavolos came other priests, lesser ones whose faces revealed unholy joy as they came down the stairs. Two of them lifted Calypso, but it took four to carry Hercules. The strong light made him blink as they emerged from the mouth of the tunnel.

Shock forced his eyes to remain open as they entered the charmed fire-pit circle. Blood-red came the sun between the two monoliths to fall upon the great Cromlech that was redder still with human gore. A wave of nausea swept up from Hercules's stomach. He fought it down. Then the strength filtered out of him as he was carried into the circle. Now he was a child in their hands. He felt himself being lifted, felt his back touch the slippery stone. Beside him Calypso was laid, the black robe she had worn ripped from her body. Diavolos' chant rose above them as the knife came up and hovered at Hercules's throat. The knife was coming down, freezing in mid air. It stopped as the air was split by the battle cry! It signaled the arrival of Hercules' crew!

As Hercules twisted his head, he saw them charge out of the woods. Like madmen, they raged across the clearing. But nobody rushed to oppose them! Instead, the Silenus priests drew back, gathered about Diavolos. As the crewmen came into the circle, the high priest's hands pulled the magic symbols out of the air. The crew stopped in their tracks like men of stone, they were, a tableau of arrested motion. There was no hope. The bitterness of gall was in Hercules's mouth as he turned his head from the scene. He looked at Calypso. Her eyes were bright, burning into his own. No hopelessness there. Her eyes were speaking to him. They were willing him, willing him to strength! Hercules felt it come back to him. Her magic was stronger than she knew. He felt the strength come back in a surge that would not be denied. This was only leather that held him. The leather could bite into his flesh as he strained. But it could not hurt him. His great chest filled with air and the thongs gave, stretched. And burst!

In a single leap, he was off the altar. He wanted to rage into the Silenus priests, to tear them apart with his bare hands, but there were too many. And Calypso's will was telling him that there was something else he must do.

He knew what it was. He had to destroy the power source. They were turning to meet his charge, setting themselves solidly. Hercules wheeled, jetted around them and then around the Cromlech. They guessed his purpose and leaped to stop him. They had to prevent him from reaching the two great stones. Hercules batted them aside, exploding through them. His back was against one of the monoliths, his feet against the other.

He climbed that way, ignoring the knives that slashed at his back. Then he was above the reach of their arms. The sun was full in his face. His shadow blocked the altar. With his back firmly braced against one stone while his feet were supported by the other stone, the two great pillars rooted in the earth strained against the strength of one man. Yet that man was Hercules. Slowly his legs straightened, his shoulders arched back. All the power that was in his muscular frame went into the thrust. It was a power that would not be denied. A pillar swayed, tottered, as it ripped out of the earth.

Hercules felt himself falling and twisted catlike in the air to land on his feet. He whirled to meet the charge of the Silenus. Diavolos' hands still traced the air, but his power was gone. The crewmen exploded into life again, their swords whirring a song of death. Only Diavolos did not lose his head. Defeated, the Silenus were and beaten, but he could snatch some measure of victory from the defeat. He was at Calypso's side when Hercules reached him. One great hand on Diavolos' throat, another at his waist, Hercules lifted him high and hurled him earthward. Diavolos twitched once and was still. The stone knife, remaining in his hand, would never be used by him again. The day of the Silenus was over.

Calypso smiled gratefully at Hercules as he cut her free. She tried to kiss him, but he pushed her away.

"I am married. Here she comes now."

Megara jogged up to the side of Hercules.

"Wow, she is a beauty," said Megara with a smile.

Alas there was no monetary treasure, but the crew had no complaints. It had been a good fight. For Hercules, that was the greatest treasure of all.

Hercules, Megara, the crew and Calypso left on their ship to finally head to the shores that would lead them onto their journey to Panemorfi.

✝✝✝

Days later, upon landing, the warrior couple said goodbye to their friends. Then they proceeded on horseback to continue their trek. The sun was out, shining as Hercules and Megara traveled down an ancient, well-worn road. One they had journeyed numerous times before, yet today if felt quite different though. While they were on their way to the Royal Palace, they became engulfed in a dust storm and soon lost their way. When the violent storm finally dissipated they resumed their journey once again yet their surroundings felt quite odd. The road seemed alien to Hercules. As Hercules surveyed the area, to his right he noticed a glistening blood-red metallic door reflecting greatly in the afternoon sun.

"Look Megara, How strange to see such a portal in the middle of nowhere."

"I don't like it, Hercules," Megara cautioned.

Hercules jumped off his horse and approached the mystifying door. He glanced back towards Megara and then examined the door. He reached out with his left hand while his right hand rested on the pommel of his sword and pushed on the door. It swung open, to Hercules surprise. He saw himself with his wife seated on her horse behind him. Hercules quickly turned around, discovering that his wife was gone. Hercules turned back and faced the opening to again see himself and his wife. Hercules stepped through the doorway to get to his wife and was launched into a dark tunnel with no visible light. He called out for Megara but received no reply. He stumbled onward, trying to see through the darkness. Gradually a light began to dimly shine further down the earthen corridor, a small round light no bigger than a pebble. Hercules walked towards this light as it started to intensify. He shielded his eyes from the glare with an upraised forearm. He again called out to Megara and again he received no reply. Then he smelled a familiar smell, that of sulfur and rot.

"The Underworld," Hercules whispered aloud.

Hercules had once again been lured into the depths of the Underworld by his Father's brother, Hades. But why? Hercules progressed further along the tunnel, coming upon a large entrance in which a skeleton was positioned that looked like nothing from his world. Draped around the skeleton was the necklace he gave to Megara years ago. The skeleton glowed as though its skeletal surface was embodied with encrusted ice crystals. The bones were obviously those of a beast that in life was partially human and partly a Daimonas bat. The creature had stood a little under five feet tall with chunky, mighty, bowed legs. The long arms ended in claw-like mockeries of hands. The skull was comparatively little, with an aggressively inclining brow and protrusive dentition. About the skeleton's neck, there was a broadband of some unknown dull metallic element, with its polished external surface roughly sketched with characters that resembled old hieroglyphs. Hercules's face was ashen with sorrow.

"Megara must be dead," he said woefully. "She would certainly never have given up her necklace willfully."

Hercules stared intently into the center of the cave without saying anything. Then he noticed a piece a parchment stuck to the necklace. He bent down and snatched the note. It was written in the hand of Megara!

Help! I'm bound captive in a Cave called Erebus! Hercules crunched the note in his hand.

Megara was still alive but in the Daimonas side of the Underworld. He had mixed emotions.

There was anger and hope in Hercules's thoughts. *There's only one way in which I may perhaps rescue her. I'll need payment to the Charon, the ferryman to the Underworld. I'll need the help of Zeus.* Hercules called out to Zeus and waited. Minutes later Hercules heard the voice of Zeus.

"Hercules, this act of violence, is not by the hand of my Brother Hades. I am not sure who is behind the kidnapping of your wife. The Underworld is hard for me to see as are all things that go on there." There was a blinding flash of light and weapons appeared at the demigod's feet. "But please take this shield and this sword. Both have the power to bring you back to your world. All you need to do is find an exit and these items will be your key. Hand them to the Charon and he'll bring you back to this world. Look for a cave that is bright in blue and violet colors which is in the Underworld Realm called Elysium. Remember Hercules no human can spend more than a day in the Underworld or they will be trapped there forever."

"I know, Father. I will find her and will get her out. Thank you for your help."

"Good luck, my son."

Hercules picked up the gold shield and sword, feeling the weight in his hands, he smiled. He knew which way to go to get to the Cave of Erebus. It is where he had fought a Cerberus many years ago. Hercules came to the spot where he knew he must enter. It would not be an easy journey for the Underworld was full of lost souls of murderers and rapists. Once he reached the Daimonas realm, it would get much harder.

He took a small step into a cave with smooth walls which were dark red in color. He remembered the stench, the smell of dead flesh and warm blood. Suddenly, a burst of energy filled Hercules body and a tingling rushed through his limbs becoming almost unbearable. He lost his vision for a moment upon returning he thought for a moment his eyes were damaged, for all he could see was red. He soon realized that the blazing color of red was a natural aspect of things in this part of the Underworld. The place was consumed in deep layered hues and shades of crimson. The surrounding rocks, bushes, trees emitted an intense heat of its bloody radiance giving the still dry air a nearly tropical temperature. From the moon's position in the sky and its size, Hercules was forced to conclude that it must be the Underworlds sun. Did they have day and night? For a moment Hercules contemplated what to do next. He had been here before but not on this side of the Underworld. He decided to abandon this passage, deciding to approach the rockier terrain. There he knew that he could find his bearings.

But to get there he had to go through dense brush. It was so dense that in order to save time and energy, he had to use a small path that was paved before him. But he would have to leave this path soon for he did not want to battle a Daimonas horde, knowing that they would also take the easier path. Hercules decided to head for the crest of one of the low dunes some fifty feet away. He moved from the path jumping over a section of the sharp brush. He moved swiftly up to the top tried trying to locate a landmark that would help him get his bearings. He must find the 'Cave of Erebus' that Megara had written about. It seemed time did exist in the Underworld. Everything moved in pattern that was foreign. Hercules walked and he tried to keep time in his head but he could not. It could have been hours or days. He knew he must just keep searching and would eventually find something that was familiar to him.

✝✝✝

Hercules came to the foot of the hill's slope, stopping to investigate his surroundings, he realized it was silent, too silent...unnaturally silent. Suddenly, as if a thousand screams all cried at once, the silence was shattered. He wondered what creatures could make such a sound. The screams swelled to a torturous decibel, turning into a pulsing sound that nearly crippled him. He covered his ears, but it did nothing to suppress the piercing cries. The sound slowly started to diminish turning into a small whistle. Hercules brought his hands down listening intently. To the right of him about one hundred yards away he saw large bats flying about. The bats were at least three feet taller than Hercules. They turned the corner and disappeared into a cave, all except one.

One of the larger bats reappeared, seeming to stop mid air, hovering above. It started to descend slowly towards Hercules. Hercules put his hand on his sword ready for action. The bat picked up speed and was now only a few feet away. As the winged creature slowed its decent, it released a piercing scream, lunging at Hercules with his fangs wide. Hercules swiftly moved aside drawing his sword from his sheathed and brought it down hard on the animal's neck. Its head flew off neatly, arcing through the air, eventually falling and rolling onto the ground like a coin being tossed to a barkeep. Hercules decided to climb the dune to reach higher ground and thus be better able to survey the surrounding area.

He put his shield on his back and began the arduous climb upwards. The climb was difficult. The red rock crumbled at his feet and his hands grabbed and pulled determined to reach the top. Hercules felt uneasy as if something was watching him climb. He remained alert as someone, or something, could be awaiting on the crest. As he neared the pinnacle, a sound startled him. He thought he could see an outline of a monstrous winged creature. Another bat creature? Without any warning came a great wind from the wings of a giant creature. Hercules dived forward but was hit in the back by the monster's tail. Luckily his shield took much of the blow. Before he could get up, the creature grabbed him by its claw-like feet and jerked him up into the air.

The wings above Hercules began to thrust and carry him higher. Hercules felt the creature loosen his grip around him as he tried to break its hold, but he could not. Now he could see the face of this monster and was repulsed by what he saw. It was a giant bat with eyes of silver and white. The creature was still climbing, and Hercules knew that if he escaped at this height, the fall would kill him. Again he looked at the creature and tried to think of a way out of his dilemma.

The wings were at least thirty feet in length. There was no fur but a red leather skin that smelled of oil and smoke. The strange thing about the beast was that it never looked at Hercules once. It was as if it was in a trance, not under its own command. Hercules' two hundred twenty-five pounds of weight must have been a problem for this monster because again Hercules felt the creature constantly having to shift its grip on him.

Finally Hercules noticed that they were starting to descend. He decided that this was his best chance to escape. His left arm went for his sword, and he drew it out of its sheath slowly, thrusting it upwards, hitting the bat creature in its thigh. The creature shrieked a horrible sound and gripped him tighter. Hercules almost dropped his sword but instead stabbed at the beast once again. This time the claw-like feet let go of Hercules.

He fell to ground twenty feet below but was not severely hurt, and he quickly looked up at the bat creature as it made a slow turn in the sky and started to come back for him. Hercules smiled and did not move. He just waited with his sword ready as he gripped both hands on the handle. The bat creature flew down and yelled with a shriek that vibrated the ground below his feet. As soon as the creature was over him, Hercules moved swiftly to his right and chopped down onto the neck the monster. The shrieking suddenly stopped. The only sound was a thud and smaller sounds as its head rolled down the hill. The creature's body flew upward and once it reached a height that Hercules could barely see it came back down crashing into the dune with a thunderous crash.

Triumphant, Hercules looked around trying to regain his bearings. He wanted to get back to the cave he where he had started his journey, but the bat creature carried him miles away from it. Now he was not certain which way to travel. He took a knee and began to scan the landscape. Hercules' ears began to hear a familiar sound. A sound of thousands of feet running faintly in the distance. His battle with the bat creature had apparently attracted Daimonas, and their number was legion.

His enemies were fast approach from every direction. Hercules rose and took a deep breath. He searched the terrain to find a clearing and decided it was much better to fight there. He sprinted over and waited tensely, reading himself to do battle. The rush of Daimonas circled him.

The red brush surrounding Hercules kept the Daimonas hidden, yet he could hear them communicating back and forth waiting for the attack. He saw them moving swiftly left to right. Hercules just stood there waiting for them to attack. The creatures quickly went silent. Hercules tensed and then out of the brush came a large red figure covered with scales. He was tall and thick. His eyes were black with white pupils. His hands were claws, and his feet resembled the same claw like features. His mouth, while small, had large sharp protruding teeth.

This Daimonas was the leader. Around the wrist of his right hand was a band that looked to be silver but Hercules could not be for sure. It did seem to resemble the band he had given Megara for her birthday the previous year. Hercules squinted and looked closely at the armband and knew it was indeed Megara's. Hercules stepped forward to address the monster. The beast responded with a shriek that commanded hundreds of the Daimonas to swarm into the clearing from every side. Hercules lifted his sword and readied himself for a bloody battle.

He knew his sword would splatter blood and brains in every direction. Another loud shrill roared from the leader, and the horde closed in. Hercules's made a massive pile of Daimonas bodies with murderous effect. Yet he still steadily handled the sheer weight of the Daimonas numbers. They were in fact legion. The Daimonas kept coming; the mass was never ending; there had to be thousands upon thousands of them. Hercules swung his sword from side to side, slashing them in half. The bodies piled up, and Hercules felt his feet start to slip in the warm blood and entrails. He knew he could not hold this pace much longer, but he kept slashing. Daimonas heads disappeared in a red mist. Death spurted from everywhere. The sword was a flash of silver spraying red left and right. Hercules wondered how long he could continue. He finally caught a large Daimonas with his sword, getting it stuck in his gut. With his hands slippery with warm blood he lost his sword, and the Daimonas fell upon him. They quickly disarmed him. They tied him with some strange metal rope and picked him up and carried him downwards.

Hercules lifted his sword and readied himself for a bloody battle.

The Daimonas carried Hercules for what seemed like miles. He knew he could break free from the strange metal rope but waited in hope they would take him to where Megara was captive. They marched on downward and came to a small cave that gave off a yellow light. They walked in still carrying Hercules. He saw the glow was produced by yellow flames coming up from a fissure in the ground. But as he got closer to the crack, he noticed it was not flames at all, but appeared to be some sort of lightening.

Hercules was dropped on the floor.

He looked around hoping to see Megara but to no avail. The only things he saw were the horde of Daimonas. They stood there looking at him. He heard a noise above him and looked up. Sitting on a crude rock was a grotesquely fat, mangy old Daimonas who was obviously the King. Some thirty or forty Daimonas, the bigger ones, obviously the warriors were in front, making noises that were supposed to scary. As Hercules was picked up and placed before the King's throne, most of them abandoned their other pursuits to come surging around the captive studying him out of curiosity. The leader of the pack that had captured Hercules presented the Daimonas-King with the captive's sword and shield and the old fat ruler took these trophies with delight. The shield and sword were promptly placed at his feet.

The King graciously gave the shield to the Daimonas who had captured Hercules and the turned his attention back to their captive. He looked Hercules up and down then gave out a loud cry. A score of the Daimonas promptly closed in upon Hercules and dragged him to a nearby cave. Near the entrance was a giant pit. Hercules looked down and saw a Cerberus, chained up and looking as if it hasn't been feed in a long while. There Hercules was released from his bonds. He made no move to take advantage of his freedom, realizing that the swarming thousands of Daimonas in the cave made an escape impossible for the moment. He allowed himself to be herded to the edge of the pit. Looking into it, Hercules smiled because at the floor of the pit seated on stones was Megara. She appeared weary but unhurt. She smiled happily upon looking up and seeing her husband.

"Hercules! Oh, thank God you've come!"

The leader of the guards motioned for Hercules to jump down into the pit. He needed no urging. Hercules dropped to the sandy floor and immediately Megara was in his arms. The Daimonas left a dozen of their number scattered as watchmen around the edge of the depression. The rest of them returned to the main horde, leaving the prisoners to their own devices.

"I knew that you'd come, as soon as you got my note," Megara exclaimed. "But how did you ever succeed in finding this Cave of Erebus?"

"I didn't find it myself," Hercules admitted. "I let them capture me. I tried fighting at first but they were thousands of them."

Megara nodded and then told him what happened to her.

"Hercules, I materialized in the Underworld almost in the middle of a group of Daimonas. They took me captive immediately. I looked around and you were not here. I tried to escape, of course," the girl continued, "but when I was brought to the cavern I saw one of the Daimonas leaving, I believed he was going to the entrance to the Underworld, so I slipped a note on him hoping you would run into him?"

Hercules confirmed he had found the note and how it had buoyed his spirits.

"What do you think they want from us?" his mate queried.

"My guess is they want me," said Hercules. "They want the power of Zeus to fight Hades. They think if they hold me prisoner they have something to bargain with Zeus."

"Who are these creatures, Hercules?"

"Demons of the Underworld. Once many and powerful thousands of years ago. But eventually they were made into slaves here on this side of the Underworld. It appears they have grown in power."

Their conversation was abruptly interrupted by a rhythmic, snarling chant from the vast horde of Daimonas in the cave above. The chant was strange, and Hercules surmised it was part of a ritual of some kind.

"They've been doing that ever since I was first brought here," Megara told him.

The chants slowly died down. Then the sound of thousands of feet were heard rapidly approaching the captured couple. A rude wooden ladder was lowered into the pit and a warrior called for them to climb up. When they reached the top, they were again tied up. There was no sign of the thousands they had heard earlier as Megara and Hercules were led out of the cave. There in front of the entrance was what Hercules believed to be a place where sacrifices were made. *This is getting ridiculous,* Hercules thought. *Twice in one week.*

The main horde of Daimonas was there now, countless thousands of them, packed in a circle. Hercules realized he'd been wrong this was not to be a ceremonial sacrifice after all. But instead he was about to be challenged to combat. The giant who Hercules thought to be their military leader was seated on a high perch looking down at them. He waved his right hand and cried out a command. Two large Daimonas came forward with weapons at ready looking to battle Hercules and Megara.

"Megara they want us to fight these two. I'll fight them, you get our weapons back from the fat King."

Megara nodded slightly in quick understanding and then Hercules, with a massive shrug, broke free of his bonds. The crowd of Daimonas all shrieked at this display of superhuman strength. He next went to Megara and tore her bonds away as well. He was wasting no time.

Hercules leaped into the air landing his right fist in the jaw of one of the charging Daimonas. It fell to the ground hard creating a giant crater that shook the area. The other creature seeing this fled away dropping his weapon, a bright silver spear. Seeing this, Megara rushed over and picked up the heavy spear. With her own impressive might, she drew back and hurled it towards the fat King missing him by mere inches. He fell back cowering in feat.

"Let's go!" Hercules shouted.

She ran up and over the wall toward the King and his bodyguard. Catching them both by surprise, neither was able to offer any serious defense. Megara kicked the fat King over and then drover her right elbow into the stomach of the startled bodyguard. She follow this with a solid fist punch to his ugly face. He collapsed with a broken neck. Moving swiftly, Megara took up Hercules' his sword and shield and tossed them to him. Snatching his sword, Hercules readied himself to fight the horde of monsters he expected to fall upon him. But they made no such movement.

Suddenly, out of the sky came a Vasilias, flapping his bat-like wings that protruded from the back of his armor. He glared at Hercules from behind his thick black horned helmet.

"I see. Finally, the true leader emerges!" Hercules declared.

The Vasilias was second only to Hades. Now it makes sense. He was the one who wanted Hades removed so that he could rule the Underworld in his stead. The Vasilias started to laugh but stooped when it beheld the countless Daimonas dead lying at Hercules' feet. The famous demigod almost looked at home amongst the dead. His arms and chest were stained red from blood of his enemies. His shield no longer showed the golden shine but now was dull with black and red. His sword was the same and Hercules at that moment swished it in the air to shake off its coating of blood and gore.

The Vasilias was attired in heavy plated silver armor which had a glossy sheen. His sword was long and curved with a serrated blade. The Vasilias finally landed softly and retracted his wings.

He faced Hercules. "You wish to challenge a master of the Underworld?"

Hercules frowned, "Hades is the ruler here! You're nothing without your army of Daimonas!"

The Vasilias paused. He lifted his arm up in the direction of the Hercules and a strange creature emerged from underground. It was black with a giant hump on its back and its mouth was filled with teeth the size of large knives. Before Hercules could see anymore of the monster, it lunged at him. He blocked its charge with his shield. With a mighty shove, he pushed the thing to the ground, then raising his sword, he reeled back and chopped of its head with one slice of his razor edged blade.

Then Hercules charged the Vasilias. He brought his sword down but his blow was blocked. Spinning around, Hercules twirled the weapon in his hand and smashed it into the Vasilias face denting his helmet and sending him flying backward. Hercules shifted his hand prepared to continue his attack but was knocked off balance when the now desperate Vasilia ordered another Daimonas enter the contest. Hercules barely had time to register his new foe before it smashed in his chest and sent him hurtling backward into the cave wall.

Hercules landed on his feet dazed. He coughed up blood, shook his head, and looked back at the Vasilias. He brought his shield up with a grunt of exertion. The Vasilias jumped up into the air and flew with his blade drawn towards Hercules to finish him. Hercules grabbed his shield and blocked him. The Vasilias bounced off the shield and landed several yards away in a heap. Hercules dropped his shield, held his sword with both hands and swung it down towards the groaning Vasilias.

The Vasilias feebly attempted to block the stroke with his left arm, but the strength of Hercules was too great. The sword went through the arm like clearing brush and stuck Vasilias' chest armor. The Vasilias quickly jumped up and shrieked causing the cave walls to vibrate. Hercules' sword was still stuck in his chest plate armor. Vasilias pulled it out and flung it to ground. Then he grabbed his severed left arm off the ground and pulled it close to his body. He stumbled back against the wall and looked up at Hercules. Both rushed each other.

Hercules yelled as did the Vasilias. They collided head on, both striking the other relentlessly. Then after a few second, they each retreated, both wounded and out of breath. Again the Vasilias took the offensive and swung horizontally at Hercules' chest while Hercules lunged with a twist of his sword that tossed the Vasilias hand to the side. Hercules countered with a stab that knocked the Vasilias back, which was followed up with a headbutt that stunned the winged warrior. Hercules followed through with a two handed overhead swing that cracked the Vasilias helmet in two. The Vasilias recovered and pushed down to propel himself high into the air. Once airborne, he summoned more Daimonas. They ran straight at Hercules and with one motion he cut them all down. Hercules threw his shield at Vasilias which surprised him. It hit the Vasilias in the chest and sent him flying into the wall. Now seriously dazed, Vasilias struggled to get up. The dent in his armor had produced a two-inch crack. He stood resolutely and glared at the Hercules.

"Interesting you are providing an even more powerful challenge then I anticipated Hercules."

Hercules sneered at his opponent. "Come, let's finish this!"

Hercules punctuated this by charging again with his sword held low. The Vasilias smiled as Hercules was suddenly stopped in his tracks. He could not move. He looked down and saw skeleton hands had grabbed his feet and legs. He cut at them with his sword. Then he looked just in time to see Vasilias coming at him. The Vasilias' blade cut through Hercules armor and into the leather below it and kept going, biting deep into his gut. Hercules grunted with pain and anger, but refused to give up. He grabbed the Vasilias sword arm with his left hand and brought his sword around from its low position to smash onto the Vasilias' side. The Vasilias tried to pull away, but Hercules would not release his grip. He held his arm tightly, swinging his sword again but this time at the Vasilias sword arm. With Vasilias' arm outstretched, the sword cut down on the elbow and removed his other arm quickly. Hercules lets go of his enemy's limb. He then swung his sword for another two-handed strike to the side of Vasilias head. The sword struck head directly under the left eye. Hercules swung so hard he cut clean through the skull killing the Vasilias instantly.

✝✝✝

With that, Hercules collapsed to the ground. The grievous wound in his gut finally breaking through his adrenaline. He stumbled back up and grabbed his sword and shield and headed for Megara. Megara screamed and pointed. Hercules turned around to see thousands of Daimonas yelling and screaming, waiting for one of them brave enough to start another attack. Hercules took the initiative and took the fight to them while Megara looked for an exit. Megara and Hercules both worked to where they needed to go slowly. He looked down at his wound and wondered if this could really be the end. The creatures followed closely and Hercules knew they were near the cave that led back to their world. Hercules slashed and killed two Daimonas. Thousands of Daimonas waited long enough, they now had many warriors with them were ready to launch one final surge to kill their hated foe. Hercules yelled a battle cry. The charge wavered momentarily. Then Hercules felt Megara tugging frantically at his arm.

"Hercules, the rocks under us are crumbling!" she cried. "We'll fall down into the pit!"

Hercules knew what was in that pit; Cerberus the three-headed dog he battled many years ago. Not the same, but one similar to it. The horde of Daimonas rallied and swept forward in a wave that nothing stop. But their charge was too late. The entire rocky projection collapsed with a final sickening lurch, and slid to the pit's floor, carrying Megara and Hercules with it in a miniature avalanche of rocky rubble. Even in the chaos of their wild descent, Hercules retained his grip upon his sword. They hit bottom and only ten feet away was the Cerberus. Hercules pushed Megara behind him and lunged forward crashing his sword into one of the animal's three heads. He had learned years ago that cutting the off of the middle head caused the others to die as well, but he missed. His injuries were to blame. The left head of the dog grabbed his sword in his teeth and flung it aside. Hercules quickly backed up to protect Megara before attacking again. Then, looking up the mound of debris, Hercules spied the exit. The doorway he and Megara needed to reach the Charon, the ferryman to and from the Underworld.

Hercules used his remaining strength and with Megara on his back climbed the rubble to reach the cave mouth. Looking down he saw the monster Cerberus tear into the Daimonas. He took Megara's hand and walked into the cave. There by a silent river was the Charon; tall and thin as he always appeared. He nodded as the two boarded his small boat. The Charon reached out his bony hand as Hercules placed the required payment in his palm in order to be taken back to the living.

Then suddenly everything else in the nightmare place of the Underworld was blotted out in a giant swirling cloud of pulsing yellow flame that seemed to sweep them bodily up into the air and whirl them dizzily around. The world they were in disintegrated around them. For what seemed like endless eons of time, Hercules and Megara traveled through a limitless universe of swirling, tinted fires, then the eddying clouds of flame began to combine and solidify with startling suddenness. A moment later, like the abrupt light of the morning sun, the mists vanished, and Hercules and Megara felt firm footing again under their feet.

Around them was the road he remembered. Megara blinked her eyes, looking around the familiar setting. She took the fresh air into her lungs. Hercules searched for the horses finding that they were still there eating in a peaceful meadow. They casually looked over towards Hercules and continued to eat. Hercules was about to say something, but Megara cut him off.

"Now tell me again how this was going to be an easy journey to Panemorfi," Megara asked with a slight smile. Hercules sighed and put his arm around Megara as they walked over to the horses.

THE END

Write What You Love

I write because it's what I love to do, it's what brings me more passion and joy than anything I've ever done in my life. Am I good at it? I don't know. But I absolutely love writing stories. I had a fun time writing the Hercules story. It was a lot harder than the zombie, werewolf and giant monster stuff I like to write. But I really wanted to tell a fun action adventure story about Hercules. I hope you like the story and if you want you can reach me on my website to talk more about it. Until then keep reading!

†††

JAMIE EVANS - is from Columbus, Ohio and is a Horror and Science fiction author. His books include, Planet of the Blood Demons, Zombie Resort, Kaiju Island, and Ceara Amena: Desert Warrior and are published by Horror Pulp Press. Jamie Evans has sold numerous short stories to a variety of magazines, e-zines, podcasts and anthologies. Prior to his emergence as a writer he started 'Dark Dossier Magazine' the Magazine devoted to the coverage of Aliens, UFOs, Ghosts, Monsters, unexplained phenomena, and mysterious events.

Visit the website: www.jamie-evans-books.com and www.darkdossier.com

NO WRATH LIKE A NYMPH SCORNED

BY JOEL JENKINS

Through the dark of night, Paris crept over the high walls and past the wary guards of King Menelaus, through the trellised gardens where grapes grew in thick clusters ripe for the plucking, and past the twisted boles of olive trees that were ancient when once Atreus, King of Mycenae, was murdered, thrust through the spleen by his trusted nephew.

Paris's feet made no sound that was not covered by the sibilant psithurism of wind murmuring through the inky vineyards. And why not? For he traveled as lightly as the wind itself, naked but for the sandals that shod his feet and for the skirt about his loins, which was girded up as if for war—for bloodshed would ensue if he was discovered here in the gardens of the King of Laconia this night.

He carried a javelin in one hand. A bronze xiphos of two-feet in length was slung from his baldric, and slapped gently against his shoulder. Other than this, Paris passed unencumbered through the gardens, the cool breeze drying the perspiration from a brow and features so high and handsome that even the most beautiful of the goddesses had once vied jealously for his approbation, and a wedge-shaped torso so striated with muscle and perfect in form that mortal women had been known to swoon in his presence.

Of these advantages he was utterly aware, but no tincture of humility tainted this noble specimen, and by promise of the goddess Aphrodite and virtue of his own supernal beauty, he ascertained the right to seize whatever he determined should be his. Thus, with no doubt of his integrity or character, he obscured his javelin amid the foliage of the ivy at the base of King Menelaus's keep, and scaled the walls to Queen Helen's chambers, where glowed an oil lantern frosted with a crimson pane, which hung in the open window.

This was the guide that Paris had followed since scaling the outer walls, and which had been a beacon as he wove his way through the garden mazes, and past the sentries upon their appointed routes. In his eagerness, Paris almost failed to notice one of these sentries passing below, as he hung midway up the wall.

A rustling in the ivy alerted the sentry, causing him to stop and lean upon his spear as he gazed up into the impenetrable mass of leaves. The waning moon revealed nothing to his eyes and there came no further rustling, so the sentry did not prolong his rounds any longer and continued on.

Once the sentry had passed out of sight, Paris let out his pent breath and resumed his climb, more deliberately now, for his haste and burning desire had caused him to become reckless. Finally, he crawled through the open window, passed the silken tapestries that flowed in the breezes and there he saw the lovely face and figure of Queen Helen.

Indeed, they were a match in beauty. For as handsome a specimen of masculinity as Paris was, so was the succulence of Helen unmatched by that of any mortal woman. Her hair was unbound, falling in lustrous waves and her skin was unmarred by even the slightest blemish so that her perfectly formed features appeared to glow as with their own effulgent fires. The bravest of heroes withered before her beauty, and indeed her list of suitors had consisted of the most valiant of heroes and kings—and in order to avoid a civil war breaking out over a decision about who she should marry, each of them was required by her father Tyndareus to sign a pledge—the Oath of Tyndareus—that they would defend the winner of the contest that would decide who would take Helen's hand in marriage.

Though wife of another man and mother of a daughter borne to him, Helen had not failed to fall to the charm of Paris, as had so many other women before—even the nymph Oenone of Mount Ida, whose supernal beauty and ability to heal the most grievous of wounds was renowned throughout Troy and its far reaching environs. Now Helen rose from her bed, clothed in a toga which molded enticingly to her graceful form, and threw herself into Paris's strong arms. They rained passionate kisses upon each other.

"I thought you should never come!" breathed Helen, between kisses.

"How could I fail to search thee out, e'en though a thousand oceans and a million men kept us apart?!" responded Paris with equally fervent a passion. "No fiend, man, or army could keep us from appointing our true love, for it is destined by the gods that we should meet."

"If only you had been among the heroes who had appointed themselves my suitors then perhaps the obstacles between us should not be so many!" gasped Helen.

"No matter," said Paris. "Come away with me this night, and our love will burn its hot flame despite how many seek to extinguish it!"

"I would follow thee to the ends of the earth, Paris!" exclaimed Helen, and she responded with such vigor to his kisses that it appeared he might be overwhelmed by his passions and hurl her upon the bed so they might consummate their lusts even in the home of her husband, but a final thimble of sanity washed away such notions in cold clarity, when he heard footsteps outside Helen's chamber.

For a moment, Paris feared it might be Menelaus himself coming to perform his duty as husband, but more likely it was the tread of a passing servant or perhaps a sentry, for the footsteps continued on down the corridor. Still, this impressed upon Paris the need to depart with the utmost of haste, else he be caught in the bedchamber of another man's wife.

"The ivy is thick upon the outer walls," advised Paris. "I will descend first and then you follow."

"But the sentry?" questioned Helen.

"He has just passed again," observed Paris, as he peered through the window. "If we act in haste, we might be able to slip by before he makes another round."

"Then go!" urged Helen. "Do not fear, I will be close behind you."

Paris negotiated the natural trellis of vines with little difficulty, and waited next to the leafy bower, watching as Helen lowered herself through the window, and admiring the graceful curve of her calves and thighs, and her callipygian beauty as she descended. He was so enthralled by this view that he did not notice the approach of a second sentry who called out to him.

"Ho, what are you doing there?" questioned the sentry.

Paris replied by plucking his javelin from amidst the ivy, where it leaned, and lunging. He pushed the spear through the sentry's heart, so that he collapsed with a short-lived gurgle. Paris put his foot upon the breast of the crumpled sentry's body and wrenched out the point of his javelin, then dragged the sentry into the grape arbor where he wouldn't readily be seen in the dark of night.

All was justified in the pursuit of love, so Helen scarcely blinked at this cold murder, not even commenting upon it when she reached the ground. "The other sentry will be around in less than two minutes. We should make all haste to your ship!"

Paris needed no further urging, and taking Helen's hand he alternately led her and she him, for she was far more familiar with these gardens than he, through the labyrinthine bowers and arbors until they reached the encompassing walls. Now, encumbered by Helen, Paris did not attempt to scale the outer wall, instead he lurched from the shadows and speared a guard who stood watch at a small postern.

He pinned the guard to the wall, twisting the spear in his lung so that he could not call out for aid, watching him writhe and die while Helen fumbled the keys away from the guard's belt and unlocked the postern.

Finally, when she had unlocked the door, Paris let the guard fall to the ground. He jerked out his javelin and put the point again through the unfortunate fellow's throat, to ensure he did not speak any final words of warning to his fellows ere he died. Paris and Helen slipped through the postern and then they were gone, fleeing through the hills and down the winding and precipitous streets that led to the harbor below, where waited with ready crew, the ship Aphrodite.

As soon as they crossed the creaking boarding plank, sailors drew it in, and lines were cast off. Sailors used oars to push away from the dock and sails went up to catch the breeze out of the harbor. Somewhere high above, from King Menelaus's keep, horns sounded as an alarm went out.

"They have either discovered your absence or discovered the bodies of those I slew," said Paris. "Pray to Aphrodite that she will lend us a swift wind and cause your husband's ships to founder as he pursues."

"My husband's ships are ill-prepared for pursuit," said Helen as they watched the island of Elafonisos shrink before their view. "But tell me why you call your ship after the goddess of pleasure rather than Poseidon, god of the sea?"

"I will tell you the tale in our quarters," said Paris, beckoning with one brawny arm. "For it involves you."

"How could it possibly involve me?" questioned Helen. "You have been here less than a week as emissary from Troy and surely your ship was named Aphrodite long before you ever considered sailing to Elafonisos."

Paris ushered Helen into his luxuriously appointed cabin, the divan which was strewn with fine linens, silken drapes, fringes with pearls. Brass targets hung upon the wall near a rack of javelins where Paris placed the one he had bloodied in the evening's kidnapping. "It was ... and I will tell you how Aphrodite became my patron goddess."

Though their passions simmered just beneath the surface, waiting to erupt, for a moment they were held in check as Paris related the tale of what had happened to him when he was naught but a farmer on Mount Ida. "All the gods and goddesses were invited when Peleus and Thetis were married, but one goddess, Eris, who is always bent on strife was not invited, and so she threw a golden apple into the wedding party, and inscribed upon its skin were the words 'to the fairest.'"

"And were you at this wedding?" questioned Helen.

"Oh, no. Not I!" replied Paris, "for I was banished to the slope of Mount Ida because Hecuba had muttered some supposed prophecy that I would be the downfall of Troy!"

"So how can you know the story is true?" demanded Helen.

"Because I saw the apple and was told the story by the three goddesses who showed it to me," replied Paris.

"You jest!" exclaimed Helen.

"And they showed me more than just the apple," said Paris, slyly. "It seems that these three goddesses naturally assumed that the title of 'the fairest' should belong to them and, when they came to an impasse over who should possess ownership of the apple, they appealed to Zeus that he judge which was the most beautiful."

"And so why did these goddesses come to you, then?" asked Helen as she perched upon the edge of the bed, a vision of loveliness so radiant.

"Because Zeus refused to make judgment and so, these goddesses picked the mortal man best equipped to be a judge of feminine pulchritude and asked him to be the judge."

"And I suppose this is where you come into the story?" teased Helen. "What makes you so qualified to be this judge?"

"You can hardly fault my judgment," protested Paris, "for do I not rightly judge you to be the most beautiful mortal that ever my eyes have set upon!"

"Then," conceded Helen, "I must admit you to be by far the most qualified judge they might have possibly picked."

"Hera, Athena, and Aphrodite appeared to me and said that I must choose which one of them was the most beautiful!"

"How could you possibly make such a decision?" asked Helen.

"That's what I said," replied Paris. "I told them that to be a fair judge I would have to view them disrobed."

Helen was shocked by this. "And did they deign comply to such a request by a mere mortal?!"

"Naturally," replied Paris, his hands spreading in a nonchalant gesture, "for their pride was at stake—and I could not resist goading them to such lengths, for when was I ever going to have the opportunity to have any goddess, let alone three, parade for me in all their divine glory?"

"Naturally," teased Helen. "And was this to be the deciding factor for the contest?"

"I spent hours studying the most minute details," admitted Paris, "but alas, though they each offered different beauties to be infinitely admired, I could not come to a decision."

"And so were Hera, Athena, and Aphrodite satisfied when you declared they must share the golden apple and the title of the most beautiful goddess?"

"Of course not," said Paris as he seated himself beside Helen, with a glimmer of a smile playing across his handsome features when he recalled his cleverness at convincing goddesses to parade in all their unencumbered glory before him and allow him the most intimate of inspection. "They were most insistent that I make a decision. So insistent, that they began to make me offers of gifts should I choose them."

Helen regarded Paris with suspicion. "So tell me, how does this story of your supernal voyeurism relate to a humble mortal such as myself?"

"Wait for a moment and you shall see," said Paris. "You shall see how you are the prize I won from this contest."

"Truly?" questioned Helen. "I cannot imagine the gods and goddesses even aware of my existence let alone having my name upon their lips. Just what gifts were you offered?"

"Hera offered to make me king over all of Greece and to the far corners of Asia," said Paris as he slipped a strong arm around Helen's supple waist. "And Athena offered me wisdom and skill in war, but it was Aphrodite's offer that most piqued my interest."

Helen lifted her face to look into Paris's eyes. "And what pray tell did Aphrodite offer you that might surpass power and might?"

"She offered me the most beautiful mortal in all the world," murmured Paris as he loosed the toga from Helen's shoulder, "and now that I hold you in my arms she has fulfilled her promise."

The winds filled the Aphrodite's sails and pushed her hard across the dark seas, the waves beating against the hull as the enraptured lovers were carried quick toward the rising walls of distant Troy. And in their selfish bliss, the week seemed to pass as if it were merely moments and soon they touched the quays along the far-running shores.

As they disembarked from the Aphrodite, a frown creased Paris's handsome visage when he saw the bathycolpian form of the raven-haired Oenone run down the docks toward him, her arms open to greet him. But when Oenone sighted the incomparably beautiful Helen with her arm tucked in Paris's and her head leaning upon his broad chest, her great joy was suddenly dashed from her features, the wine of her happiness souring to vinegar as if before the heat of the noonday sun.

Great sobs of anguish wracked her bosom, and she went to her knees, clutching at Paris's tunic as she fell. "Tell me, beloved, that my eyes deceive me! Tell me you have not brought home a woman to take my place in your bed! Tell me that in your short absence your feelings toward me have not grown chill and that your heart has turned to another!"

Helen coldly appraised the lovely mountain nymph, daughter of the river-god Cebren and mortal woman. "Who is this wench who dares accost you thus?"

"She is nobody," said Paris, casting aside Oenone. "My past was wiped clean like a piece of slate the moment I laid eyes upon you, Helen. All remembrances of past loves were swept away in the fierce storms of my devotion to you and I am a new man, wholly yours and without the encumbrances or even the shades of former lovers."

"Then she is nothing to you," said Helen.

"She is nothing to me," agreed Paris, as he brushed aside his wife and mother of his young son. "As you have forsaken your former flames, so have I extinguished mine and renounced my former affiliations."

"But what of your son?!" demanded the nymph Oenone.

In truth, her beauty was radiant and men had been driven to the edge of their sanity when in chance they had crept upon her while she bathed in the steaming mountain springs of Mount Ida. Still, the radiant and supernal beauty of Oenone seemed wan and pale in the effulgent rays of Helen's overwhelming pulchritude.

"What son?" spoke Paris with so cold a heart that it might have turned the hot springs to ice. "I renounce you and any offspring who has passed your loins. Now, move aside or I shall cast you like jetsam into the sea."

"You foolish wretch of a man," sobbed Oenone. "This path will lead to your ruin and should you not send this unfaithful harpy back to her master, right now, your life and the life of thousands of others will be the cost!"

"My life," scoffed Paris. "How shall my life be the cost of enduring love?"

"Heracles shall prove your undoing. Heed my words, Paris! Heed my words, Paris! Put her back on the Aphrodite and send her home to Menelaus with a peace offering of gold and pearls, else the whole world be laid to waste!"

"Heracles is long dead and the citizens of mighty Troy fear no man or army!" replied Paris. "Now away with you, gutter snipe, or I shall use the flat of my blade to cause you to regret your mean words and lying prophecies!"

With the savage and anguished cries of Oenone rending their ears, Paris and Helen continued down the quay where they mounted into the chariot that Oenone had used to rush from the city, when from the walls of Troy she had, with her far-seeing eyes, spotted the Aphrodite as it hove over the distant rim of the world.

The chariot driver cast a glance toward Oenone who was still upon her knees, tearing at her raiment in anguish.

"Go!" ordered Paris. "Your new mistress stands with us in this chariot."

The chariot driver did not seem pleased at this pronouncement, for Oenone was much loved by him and all the servants of the household, but he knew better than to defy an order of his master. So he touched his whip, lightly, to the back of the horses and they began to pull the chariot up the long and winding roads toward the high walls and gleaming gate of Troy, the portcullis of which was lifted to accommodate for the constant flow of merchants in and out of the city and to the busy port below.

†††

The wrath of Menelaus would not be deterred, and he called upon the great Greek warriors who had once vied for the eburnean hand of Helen and sworn to her father the oath of Tyndaleus, that they would defend and stand with whosoever won fair Helen in marriage. So it was not before spring's end that the first prow of a thousand Achaean ships furrowed Troy's verdant shores, and the enemy warriors swept out, smiting down the Trojan defenses and, time after time, chasing them all the way to the walls of Troy, which by the grace of the gods stood firm against the bloody sieges.

Oenone retreated to a high tower in the distant hills where she became a recluse, living bitter in her sorrow, and gazing from its crenellated top, her farseeing vision tracking the wars and watching for any sign of her estranged husband, and praying for his demise, though she could not bear to lift a hand against him—for she still harbored a secret love in her shattered heart. Never did she leave the tower, sending her son out to hunt for goat in the high clefts of Mount Ida, and to gather vegetables from the gardens.

On the other hand, Helen watched the battles from the besieged walls of Troy itself, marvelling with pride at the awesome conflict that her matchless beauty had wrought. Still, as the great heroes she had known of days of old began to fall, she realized that none were immune to the sword. And when she saw the mighty Achilles, moving swiftly through the hosts, slaying Trojan with every thrust of his spear, smiting down common soldier and Trojan hero, alike, with each swing of his mighty xiphos, she worried that one day Paris might not return from his forays outside the walls of Troy—and so she prayed fervently to Aphrodite for her husband's safety, sacrificing upon her altars, and burning sweet smelling incense so that Paris might be preserved from the spear of Achilles. And twice when facing Menelaus and then Diomedes, Aphrodite spirited Paris away when sword or spear might have slain him.

Then in restless slumber, alongside of Helen, Paris dreamed a dream in which he was awoken from his slumber, as a pinprick of light shone in the darkness of his chamber, buzzing like a bee, which grew louder and mightier in his ear until it became a roaring cacophony.

Paris glanced at Helen, who lay naked in her bedsheets beside him, her hair arrayed across her pillow as if in a portrait of a masterful painting, but she was not aroused by the bombardment of sound. He looked again at the glowing prick of light, which seemed a firefly loose in the chamber. As he gazed upon this firefly it expanded in proportion, becoming the form of a woman arrayed in bright robes of unknown colors beyond his imagining. This form glowed forth bright rays of light that painted every wall, niche and corner in brilliance, and as Paris slitted his eyes against the blinding radiance, he could make out the supernal lovely features of the goddess Aphrodite.

"To what do I owe your visit?" asked Paris, "oh, great goddess Aphrodite."

"Thus far I have been a protection against the swords and spears of the Achaeans," replied Aphrodite, her voice resonating in his very being. "But the gods are divided and if this war is not brought to a close soon, doubtless Athena or some other goddess who is jealous of my beauty or a god who is jealous to possess me, will imbue some Achaean hero with the ability to strike you down and I will not be able to save you—for Zeus himself commands me that I may no longer act to preserve your life."

Paris was the most handsome of men, but he had chosen Aphrodite's gift of the love of the most beautiful woman in the world and not Athena's gift of skill and wisdom in war. "Then how shall I face the Achaean's most mighty heroes such as Diomedes, Menelaus, Odysseus, Ajax, and Achilles? My own brother, the mighty Hector, could not stand against Achilles—so what chance have I? You have granted me the love of the most beautiful mortal in all the world, but what good is the gift if I cannot keep her?"

This form glowed forth bright rays of light that painted every wall in brilliance...

Aphrodite shrugged the perfect slope of her shoulders. "Should the gods figure every jot and tittle of mortals' lives for them? There are unintended results every time the gods meddle. When I tie a thread between you and Helen, a thread elsewhere becomes unravelled. There are those close to you who are jealous that you have stolen Helen's heart, and would find a way to undermine that love."

"Nothing can destroy our love," said Paris.

"And so thought Oenone of your love before you departed for Mycenae. One thread of the tapestry knits together, and another unravels."

"Am I at fault for reaching out and grasping what you promised me?" questioned Paris.

"There is no reckoning the heart's desire, and it is inevitable that one heart should break when two are united."

"What do you mean?" asked Paris.

"I mean that love is inherently selfish. Were you thinking of Oenone, the love of your youth, when you first laid eyes upon Helen? No, you forgot her with swiftness and did not think upon her again until you strode down the quays of Troy and saw her awaiting you. Do you think upon her these years since—the mother of your son?"

"And why should I?" said Paris. "I'm sure Oenone thinks little enough of me."

"But there you would be wrong," said Aphrodite. "Every night she prays to Zeus for vengeance and then her heart softens and she beseeches me that you might be returned into her arms."

"She'd best decide on one or the other," said Paris, unfeeling. "She can't have both prayers answered."

"Can't she?" replied Aphrodite, cryptically, and then she continued. "When I blessed your union with Oenone other men's hearts were rent asunder to see their dreams dashed. One man threw himself from the cliffs and his body was broken in the sea and another's mind was so broken that it was at the utmost of his ability to drag himself onto the street to beg alms. So, you see, the wreckage that one man and one woman's love leaves in its wake."

"There is nothing I can do to change the past," said Paris, "nor would I, if given the opportunity." He looked upon the beauty of Helen; perhaps it paled in comparison to the supernal luminescence of Aphrodite. "I've made my bed and I intend to lie in it."

"Yes you will," agreed Aphrodite. "And I cannot help but wonder if greater gods than I have brought these things to a pass so that the great heroes of humanity might be extinguished, because they grow too bold and forget their makers."

Paris did not comprehend this, for he was too enrapt in his own thoughts and smaller concerns. Aphrodite saw this self-absorption and snapped her fingers. "Now, hearken closely unto me, Paris, for I shall be able to aid you one last time."

"I am hearkening," said Paris, "and I thank thee for thy aid!"

Aphrodite's robes flowed in billowing waves as she strode, her dainty feet not deigning to touch the terrestrial floor, a foot above the floor, across the chamber and to the wall where Paris's bow and quiver of arrows hung. She laid her finger upon the bow and then upon each of the arrows as if imbuing them with the mystical powers that radiated from her limbs and body.

"Perhaps you have observed Achilles in battle," said Aphrodite, her voice working up lustful thoughts in Paris's fervid mind so that he found it difficult to concentrate on the words she spoke.

"I ... yes, of course. Sword and spear slide from him like rain from a behemoth's back. No blow can pierce his skin."

"It is because he was dipped in the river Styx when he was but a child," said Aphrodite. "The only spot upon his body which is vulnerable is the very heel where he was held when he was submerged. If you can strike his left heel, deeply with an arrow, you may slay him—and I have blessed your arrows that they will mortally wound any whose flesh they pierce."

"You have given me the secret," hissed Paris. "The secret to Achilles' invulnerability!"

"Yes," said Aphrodite, the word falling like ringing timbrels from her ruby red lips. "And I have given you the means to slay the Achaean's mightiest hero from afar. Accomplish this feat and all shall fear you—both Achaean and Trojan! The Achaeans will tremble and be affrighted and perhaps you will be able to break them, send them howling back to their fortifications."

"Then on the morrow, I shall slay Achilles!" breathed Paris.

"It will be an astounding feat," said Aphrodite, "but I am no goddess of war. Am I not a goddess of beauty and pleasure?! Make propitiation for the act you will commit tomorrow by wringing cries of ecstasy from your wife's lips one more time this evening, so that on the morrow you may be forgiven for the blood you shed upon the field."

With these final words, Aphrodite's fair form diminished, the brilliant light that shone into every corner and devoured every shadow, shrinking to the size of a firefly, which for a few moments buzzed about the room and then winked out, gone, as if she had never appeared within the chamber.

Paris waited the long moments it took for his eyes to adjust to the resumed darkness, and then he found his fair wife among the sheets.

When the rosy fingers of dawn spread through the darkling sky, chasing away the shadows of the firmament, Paris arose from his bed, girded a skirt about his waist and climbed his father's palace tower so that he might overlook the landscape, the blades of the sward red from all the blood they had drunk over the years of strife and turmoil since he had absconded with fair Helen.

Here, he watched the Greeks move behind their walls built of the hulls of ships they had torn asunder when they had sworn oath not to leave until Helen was returned to their custody. They were gathering their forces to assail the ever-standing walls of Troy. While Paris contemplated the positions of the Greeks' forces, he heard the scrape of footsteps behind him.

He reached for his xiphos, but found that he had left it behind in his bedchamber, leaning against the bedstead where still Helen slumbered.

The newcomer, a man with harsh, staring eyes and unsubtle expression laughed at this reaction. "What is wrong, Paris? Do you fear treachery even within the walls of Troy, and from your own brother, even?"

"Nay, Deiphobus," replied Paris as he realized who had crept upon him in the tower, "but it was foolish for me to leave aside my blade."

"A woman as lovely as Helen is bound to cause distraction," replied Deiphobus. "You'd do well to keep your sword always girded lest you be slain and some other deserving man take up the mantle of her husband and protector."

"Already Helenus tried to steal her from me!" spat Paris. "And then you as well!"

"But we can hardly be blamed," said Deiphobus. "He thought you slain by Diomedes—a spear cast through you. And then I saw Menelaus smite you into the very dust from which you were created! How could we have known that Aphrodite snatched you away?"

"Is Helenus not a prophet?" retorted Paris. "Could he not have prophesied my return or the fact I was not slain?"

"Perhaps it behoved him to keep his prophecies silent so that he might seize your wife and spend a few nights with her before your miraculous return," suggested Deiphobus. "Now listen carefully, for Helenus is not the only man made a fool because of the beauty of a woman."

"Say what you mean," demanded Paris.

"I mean that even the vaunted Achilles, hero of the Achaeans, has been known to play the fool for a woman and perhaps we have the means to lure him to his death. I have an idea that came to me in a dream—surely from the gods, but I know not which of them has been kind enough to haunt my dreams with their divine visions."

Now, Paris became alert. "Aphrodite?"

"It seems to me that I surely would have recalled had the goddess of beauty deigned visit my bedchamber, but no matter—perhaps it was Aphrodite and she did not fully reveal herself to me. Not all of us can be so divinely favored to view three goddesses in all their unbewrayed glory!"

"And what did your dream tell you?" questioned Paris.

"The dream led me to believe that if we could lure Achilles out of the pack that you, dear brother, might have the means to slay him," said Deiphobus. "It seemed foolishness, for no one has had the might to stand before him—not even our beloved Hector."

"It is not foolishness," said Paris, "for I have received a vision this night as well and my quiver has been touched by Aphrodite!"

"Then you shall slay him with arrows when we lure him out," said Deiphobus.

"And just how will we lure him out?" questioned Paris. "My dream did not reveal that. Hold! You do not mean that I should expose Helen without the walls of Troy!"

"And why not?" taunted Deiphobus, "is she not the cause of all our woes and misfortunes? If you had been satisfied with Oenone, who is so blindingly beautiful that she hides her visage in the cliff towers beyond the city, so that she might not drive men mad, then none of this woe would have come upon Troy. Our brothers, Hector and Troilus would yet be alive and so would thousands of our bravest warriors—yet you, in your act of hubris, decide the best act of diplomacy would be to steal the wife of one who would have ostensibly been our friend and ally, and in one fell action turned the might of many nations against us!"

"Helen was promised to me of Aphrodite!" protested Paris. "Who am I to deny the will of the gods?!"

"Of one goddess," Deiphobus reminded him. "Who is to say what the other gods and goddesses will? Nevertheless, they have revealed to me how to lure out Achilles—and despite my taunts, we will not use Helen, for she should draw the whole of the Achaean armies, and our desire is only to bring Achilles."

"Then whom do you suggest we dangle as bait?" questioned Paris.

"Why our own fair sister, Polyxena," replied Deiphobus. "Perhaps, because she is your sister, you have been blinded to her charms, but not so, Achilles. For did he not spare her life when he caught she and Troilus stealing to the fountains to draw water?"

"He did not show Troilus any mercy," said Paris.

"Nay, but he was not so lovely to look upon as Polyxena," replied Deiphobus.

"We shall use our own sister as bait?" questioned Paris.

"And why not?" answered Deiphobus, coldly. "You did not hesitate to endanger the entirety of our family and people when you kidnapped Helen from her still-warm bed, why should you hesitate to risk your sister's life now? Besides, all of us are lost unless we slay Achilles, and Polyxena will be anxious to take part in this ruse—for the horror of seeing Troilus slain by Achilles' spear, before her own eyes, is still fresh in her memory, and she will be hungry for a chance at vengeance."

Paris nodded slowly as he considered his brother's words. "Then let her take another trip to the fountains to draw water, but we shall be waiting in hiding when, this time, Achilles comes for her."

"Verily," agreed Deiphobus, "and though I will not fail to put my trust in your arrows, which have been poisoned by the touch of Aphrodite, I suggest we bring a phalanx of mighty warriors—for Achilles will not be on the field of battle alone."

✝✝✝

While the rosy luster of the morning sun spread its ruddy hues upon the landscape, the lovely Polyxena, scarcely seventeen years of age, but with the prepossessing wisdom of a centenarian lurking in those crystal blue eyes, left the safety of Troy's walls, carrying a water jug upon her shoulder. She was slender and comely, the vision of her mother in her youth, and her fair hair, strewed with mingling shades of brown and blonde, fell in waves to her waist.

Though she moved quickly through the morning light, Deiphobus and Paris expected she would be spotted by the pickets upon the lapped strakes of the Achaeans walls, which bordered the shores of Troy.

However, Deiphobus and Paris did not make their exit so obvious, slipping out a covert at the rear of Troy with a contingent of tribesmen, not eunuchs like those impressed to guard the comely temple nephanims, but drawn from the giants who lived in the hills and cliffs outside of the city. Each of these stood nearly seven feet in height and carried a spear a cubit longer than the shafts of Trojan or Achaean, and some even carried axes, for the tribesmen were renowned woodsmen and some were expert with hatchet and axe.

They slipped through the rocky paths alongside the cliffs that backed the city of Troy, and as they traveled Paris couldn't help but glance into the face of the lifting sun and regard the squat tower that rose along the cliff's edge, and for a moment he imagined the curvaceous figure of his former wife, the mountain nymph Oenone standing in the crenellated gaps and watching his progress through the mist strewn paths illuminated by dawn's feeble light.

And perhaps this was no feat of imagination, for was she not the daughter of Cebren the river god, and along with the gift of prophecy, supernal beauty, and ceaseless youth, did she not possess the gift of farseeing—was she not able to read the legend scriven on the wall of a ship's hull from thirty leagues away? If so, surely she could see his vainglorious attempt to ambush Achilles, and how he was risking his own sister's life to accomplish the deed.

Perhaps Oenone was even now praying for his death or, as Aphrodite had suggested, praying that he would for some reason unbeknownst to him, cast aside the love of Helen, the woman Aphrodite had promised to him, and come crawling back, begging for her forgiveness.

Despite Deiphobus's callous demeanor, he was not unaware of the thoughts of others, and easily divined what Paris was thinking. "Do you see the nymph there in the crenels as well?"

"I do," said Paris. "She is watching for us to succeed or fail."

"And which is she hoping for?" questioned Deiphobus.

"She loves Polyxena as if she were her own sister," replied Paris, "and that will not change no matter how much she may despise me. She will not want to see Polyxena come to any harm."

They reached the rocky fountain overlooked by a statue of the muscular Cebren, who arose from the center of the fountain in a spray. In the surrounding grove of trees, they took positions of hiding behind boulder and trunk. Ere long they saw the pretty Polyxena swaying up the path from the opposite direction. Without pausing to look about her, to determine whether or not her brothers and protectors had yet arrived, she moved directly to the edge of the fountain, first dipping her fingers in the crystalline waters and sucking off the droplets, and finding them sweet to the taste.

Then she held back her long, flowing tresses to keep them from being wetted in the bubbling fountain and she pushed her lips into the water, drinking deeply of the life-giving elixir. Finally satisfied, she wiped her plump limps with the back of her arm and thrust her earthen jug into the waters, so that it bubbled and chortled as it filled.

During this entire process, Polyxena showed such prepossession that she did not even glance over her shoulder or betray, for that matter, any indication of concern or worry that the enemy might come upon her. This was made all the more remarkable, since it was not many steps from here that she and Troilus had been caught, and Achilles had put Troilus to the spear.

Indeed, from behind the boulder where Paris waited, arrow nocked upon string, he could see shadowy forms moving through the dawn light, flitting from tree to tree, and then he caught glimpses of sweating flesh, leather harnesses, helm, and bracer, in the spears of sunlight that stabbed through the leafy canopy.

Paris recognized Achaean arms and armor, and he knew that the enemy was about to arrive, and cast themselves upon the apparently oblivious Polyxena, so he signaled Deiphobus and the hill men, whose long limbs were folded into incongruous spindles as they attempted to conceal themselves behind tree and rock.

Now, Paris sighted Achilles, marvelous of limb and mien, with a haughty expression and brutally handsome demeanor that rivaled even that of Paris. His hair was long and golden and he wore armor that had surely been forged by Haphaestus, blacksmith of the gods. He moved with a quickness and surety that was so swift the eye could hardly follow, and so even though Paris had spotted him well down the path, he was surprised to see him dart into the clearing and grab Polyxena by a handful of her thick and beauteous hair, upsetting her jug of water.

"Aah, foolish woman, but one so lovely to behold," said Achilles as his sword moved toward Polyxena's long and graceful neck. "What error in judgment brings you back to the very spot where your brother was slain just one year ago?"

"Slain by you!" spat Polyxena. "I have not forgotten your cruelty!"

"Your brother was no drooling child, and he lifted a sword against me," said Achilles. "Should I have paddled him and sent him back to your mother, as I sent you? And you are no child any longer, Polyxena. You have bloomed this past year. Tell me, just what should I do with you?"

The ten Achaeans who accompanied Achilles chuckled at this comment and regarded Polyxena with lustful eyes, though they had no hope of partaking for Achilles was notoriously selfish with his slaves and concubines—after all, had he not withdrawn from the battle when Agamemnon took away Briseis, whom he had captured from Troy, putting his own desires above the welfare of all the Achaean army? Still, they reveled vicariously, for even being in the presence of a man such as Achilles made them feel powerful.

Polyxena pulled her feet beneath her skirts, so that Achilles was not dragging her along the earth. "I am no Briseis, Achilles. You will not possess me as you possess her. I should die rather than fall into your hands."

"Then die," said Achilles, "for you are already in my hands and I will do with you what I will—and do not think I do not know you. You are beloved daughter of King Priam and Queen Hecuba. Methinks you are a fine prize and that your mother and father might be more than willing to trade you for one Helen of Sparta."

"They call her Helen of Troy, now," replied Polyxena, delaying Achilles so that there might be time for her brothers and their woodsmen to spring their trap. Even now, Achilles' ten men were lured farther into the grotto where the fountain bubbled. They encircled her like wolves, anxious to see what might befall her at the hands of Achilles.

"She will never be of Troy," spat Diodotus, one of Achilles' lackeys, who eyed Polyxena with a keen interest. "Such beauty could only be of Sparta."

"And yet she was lured away by my brother and nothing King Menelaus could do would hold her," mocked Polyxena.

Diodotus raised a hand to smite Polyxena. If he had not, the shaft intended for Achilles surely would have smote him in the face. Instead, the arrow from Paris's bow pierced Diodotus's palm. The poison or deadly magic with which Aphrodite had imbued the arrows in the quiver worked immediately, and Diodotus fell to the ground, every limb unstrung, and his eyes rolling into his head.

Achilles cried out as the giant woodsmen of the hills rose up from hiding, unfolding themselves from behind trees and boulder and launching a storm of spears. "We are ambushed!"

Half of Achilles' men dropped in that first hail of spears, smote through and writhing in the dust. Polyxena wrested a hidden dagger from her girdle and stabbed Achilles in the arm with such fierce strength that the dagger broke upon his golden flesh, but the sharp point did naught but scratch his

"I should die rather than fall into your hands."

skin, for the waters of the River Styx had made him invulnerable.

Achilles gave a mocking laugh and cast Polyxena aside. "I see you are not so naïve as you pretend, fair Polyxena. Nonetheless, I will teach you a lesson in the ways of this cruel world once I dispose of these giants you thought to set upon me!"

Paris drew back his bow again, but Achilles moved so swiftly that the arrow glanced from the Achaean's calf, not leaving the slightest of scratches for Aphrodite's deadly magic to work. Deiphobus leaped from hiding and smote the spear of an Achaean in half with his xiphos, and then cleaved that warrior's helm and skull in twain.

In the meantime, the giant hill men, moved forward with spear and axe. Two of them went down beneath the spears of the Achaeans, but Achilles men could not break free of the cordon which had been thrown around him, and they were hewed down by axes, and so it was only a few bloody moments before Achilles was the only one of his party left.

Still, Achilles was renowned for his battle prowess. Each time he set foot on the battlefield he slew a dozen men, and so though he was the last Achaean standing in the clearing, the others dead or wallowing in their own blood, the conclusion was by no means foregone. He moved with the swiftness of an adder, striking through one of the hill men with his spear, ducking beneath the falling axe blow of the dying giant, and disemboweling the hill man behind him.

Dodging a spear cast, Achilles whirled around, plucking up the quivering shaft and returning it with might and main at its owner, so that the point passed through the giant's neck, bursting out the back in an arterial spray.

Deiphobus launched his spear with all the power in his frame and it smote Achilles at the joints of his armor, but though the point penetrated the seams, it did not pierce the flesh that stretched taut and as hard as bronze beneath. Still, the impact of Deiphobus's mighty attack staggered Achilles, so that he lurched forward on unsteady feet into the reach of a hill man, who brought his axe down upon Achilles' helm.

The helm, wrought by Haphaestus in his supernal forges, did not split asunder, but was instead knocked from Achilles's skull, so that his fair hair spilled out in writhing trails. Achilles reeled, stunned by the mighty blow, and Polyxena scrambled past her upended pitcher, through the legs of an advancing hill men, and sought the protection and shelter of the surrounding rocks.

The hill man pounded Achilles twice more with blows that would have rent a lesser man into pieces, but the blows never pierced his brazen and invulnerable flesh. The Achaean spat out a mouthful of blood, rose and thrust his xiphos into the giant's spleen, and then he fled the clearing, running with the speed of the wind.

"Hah!" mocked Polyxena, calling after him. "Never have I seen a coward flee the field of battle with such speed!"

"Let Apollo guide your arrow!" cried Deiphobus to Paris. "Aphrodite has given you the poison to slay him, now let Apollo be wings to your shaft!"

Paris drew back his bow and let a shaft fly; it flickered through the bloody morning light and shivered to pieces upon Achilles's hauberk.

"Another!" shouted Deiphobus. "You have time for just one more shot before the coward disappears over the crest!"

With all his strength, Paris stretched again his bow and fired another shaft, muttering a prayer to Apollo and Aphrodite as it left his string. He watched it fly straight, and too high, so that it appeared it might pass over Achilles' head but, at the last moment, it fell like a wounded duck, the hand of Apollo altering its course, so that it plunged directly into Achilles' left heel.

Achilles gave out a horrible cry as black blood spurted from his heel, leaving a trail of blood to mark every step. Still, he did not fall, he lurched toward the battle where the Achaeans pressed hard against the walls of Troy, and were cast back time and again.

Achilles smote down seven men, both Trojans and Achaeans, before he fell into the churned and bloody earth, and gave one final cry that caused his entire body to spasm as he died. Then, seeing their champion had died, the Achaeans fell back toward their walls of ship hulls and jutting masts where flew the flags of each of their combined nations.

The armies of Diomedes and Odysseus covered the retreat of the armies, and for long moments Helen could see, from the walls of Troy, those two mighty warriors who she knew of old, and who had once sued for her hand in marriage, as they threw down mighty Trojan warriors and kept the Achaean retreat from turning into a route which would have driven them all back into the bosom of the sea over which they had crossed so many years ago.

King Priam turned his bearded and hoary face toward Helen and thought perhaps he saw a gleam in her eye. "Do you glory to see so much bloodshed done in your name, my daughter-in-law?"

"What other woman in all the history of the earth has seen thousands of deeds, both noble and foul committed in her name?" wondered Helen, whose outward beauty had not diminished in its eburnean luster the slightest during these long years of siege. "What other woman could call forth a thousand ships, without speaking, to retrieve her from across the wine red seas?"

"Indeed," said King Priam. "What other woman ..."

"But though my vanity is pricked and I see all the deeds done in my name, do I possess a single iota of power to halt the bloodshed? Though it may have been my face that started the machines of war moving, I have no power to stop them, and I fear that I may be crushed in the inexorable tread of the armies that have been of my own making."

"Do you really give your powers so little credit?" questioned King Priam.

"Send me back, then," pleaded Helen. "Send me back to King Menelaus so that this war may be stopped and no more blood will be shed!"

"Do you love Menelaus?" questioned King Priam.

"Never have I loved him," said Helen. "My beauty is a curse and I was merely a prize to the winner of the contest. My father bargained me away."

"But still you would go back to him?" pressed King Priam.

"Yes, if it would stop this bloodshed," replied Helen.

"And what of my son? What of Paris?"

"I love him with all of my heart," said Helen, "but look what carnage our ardor has wrought! I would that he would have listened to Oenone, and Paris had sent me back with a hold full of gold and pearls to mollify Menelaus—and then these thousands would not have died."

"Would that I had forced him to do the same," said Priam, "instead of giving free rein to his lusts and whims. Oenone was a steady rudder in Paris's life and you have brought nothing but mercurial winds and disaster."

"Even I can see that," replied Helen. "So lower me from the walls and let us end this thing."

"It is too late for that," said King Priam. "If we bow to the demands of the Achaeans now, they will think us weak and raid our shores forever more. The die is cast and we rely on the strength of the gods to defend us, or the whim of the gods to cast us into ruin."

The morning wind whipped at Helen's lustrous hair. "See, I am powerless to stop the bloodshed. You have proven me right."

"So what will you do?" questioned King Priam.

"I will stand upon the walls and sorrow in the power my beauty has to bring men to their destruction all while taking pride in my matchless beauty that causes them to hurl themselves to their dooms, and loving your son with all the fervor of my heart."

"I will take consolation in Achilles' death," replied King Priam. "The gods have struck a blow for us and if Helenus is right, the requirements of the gods are too steep for the Achaeans to defeat us now."

"And what are those requirements?" questioned Helen.

"The gods speak that in order for the Achaeans to throw down Troy they must recover the bones of Pelops, induce the son of Achilles to come to battle, find the bow of Heracles, and have custody of the Pallas of Athena."

Helen considered this, for she knew something of how the Pallas of Athena had been spirited away in a most violent fashion. "All four of these things together are very unlikely to come to pass. Perhaps the gods will soon bring this war to an end."

"Perhaps," answered King Priam, with a glimmer in his eye.

†††

Those dreams of bringing the war to a quick end were dashed as the summer failed, bringing chill winds and raging tempests upon the wind-brined seas. The Achaeans withdrew behind their lines, more interested in revelries and contests than assailing the walls of Troy—ships came and went bringing supplies or on other mysterious missions. The embodiment of Athena on earth went missing from the temple, stolen away by two mysterious men, who Helen knew to be Odysseus and Diomedes who had crept beneath the city walls.

And then from Troy's high walls, using a spyglass, she had seen them depart on the Far Traveler on some unknown errand, even while King Menelaus went away on some voyage to distant lands. Helen prayed to Aphrodite that he would never return, but when he inevitably did, he carried a bag of bones, which he spilled on the boards of the ship to show the Achaean kings.

Then, when the Far Traveler came back from its distant voyages, Helen gave a start when she saw the man who came to the rail near the wily Odysseus.

"What is it?" asked King Priam, who took his daily walk upon the walls.

"It is Achilles!" she gasped. "He stands on the deck of the Far Traveler next to Odysseus!"

"Nonsense," said Priam as he took the spyglass. "Paris slew him with the arrows blessed of Aphrodite. I watched him die from this very wall!"

Priam peered through the glass and his mouth fell open, for it did indeed appear that the striking likeness of Achilles strode the deck.

"Did I not tell the truth?" exclaimed Helen.

"Verily, thou didst," replied Priam as he examined the imperious and handsome visage of the man, "but he is too young to be Achilles risen from the dead or saved from the grave as Aphrodite saved Paris."

"Don't speak of those days when I was given to Deiphobus to wife!" spat Helen. "Am I forever to be inherited like chattel from brother to brother?"

"Take care then that Paris does not draw nigh again to death," said King Priam, "for my sons are wilful and seize what they desire, but you should know that."

"I was not seized by Paris," said Helen, "I came of my own free will, fleeing a loveless marriage."

"But still, he took what belonged to another man," replied King Priam. "Remember, it is only Paris's life that keeps you again from Deiphobus's bed. For he won't hesitate to take you again, should Paris fall."

"Why do you torture me with stories of Paris's death?" questioned Helen.

"Because that is not Achilles on the Far Traveler—that is his son Neoptolemus. I fear that Helenus's prophecies are coming to pass and that Troy may yet fall."

"Then the bones that Menelaus scattered upon the deck of his ship?"

"Perhaps the bones of Pelops," said King Priam. "And you know that the Achaeans now possess the Pallas of Athena—you ignored the presence of Diomedes and Odysseus inside the city walls because of your anger over being given to Deiphobus when we thought Paris dead, and because of it they fulfilled yet another of the prophetic conditions required to bring about the downfall of Troy."

Helen did not deny this, for she had pierced the beggarly disguises of the two Achaean heroes when she had encountered them upon the road under the guard of Deiphobus's soldiers. Still, she had not imagined they intended to force the gates of the temple and enter the holy sanctums of Athena to steal away the Pallas, or perhaps she might have reconsidered ignoring their presence. Or perhaps she might not have, for the fall of Troy might be suitable vengeance for the ill treatment she had received when it was thought Paris was moldering beneath the earth.

But now that Paris was alive, she did not wish such a fate to come upon Troy. Perhaps if Deiphobus should come to an untimely end, she would shed no tears, but she knew of no way to bring about his demise—except to pray to Aphrodite that one of the Achaean spears might smite him, should the Achaeans leave off from their feasting and contests long enough to challenge again the Trojans who were locked safely in the impregnable walls of their city.

"They do not have the bow of Heracles yet," commented Helen.

"How should we know?" questioned King Priam. "Is the bow of Heracles marked with his name emblazoned upon the yew of its blades and, if it were so, would our eyesight be keen enough to distinguish it even through this glass? Only the far sight of Oenone could tell us such a thing."

"I do not want to hear her name spoken again in my presence," said Helen with a jealousy truly vehement for one who had caused the bathycolpian nymph to be cast aside as so much dross.

"I am sure she feels much the same about you," replied King Priam, evenly. "But if only there were a peace between us, we could use her skill of sight and prophecy so that we might preserve Troy."

"We don't need that trollop," replied Helen. "We have Aphrodite and Apollo fighting our battles, why should we need the half-breed daughter of Cebren, whose power wanes to feeble spasms should he ever step from the waters of the rivers to which he is confined?"

"I reject the help of none of the gods," replied King Priam as he observed the movement of the Achaeans. "It appears our enemy is stirred with renewed vigor. I must go review our own troops and make sure all is in readiness, should the Achaeans, in the next few days, be roused from the drunkenness of their feasting and again assay the walls."

"And why have you become so timid that you have not taken initiative during their drunkenness?" questioned Helen, "and fallen upon them while they are at a disadvantage?"

"You speak with foolish lips, woman," replied King Priam. "Thrice we have chased the Achaeans back to the shores, but those makeshift walls made from the hulls of their ships have thrice resisted us. Why should I throw good lives away after bad? Would you risk your husband on such a venture?"

"No," admitted Helen after just a moment's consideration.

"Go to him now and tell him our enemy grows restless," ordered King Priam. "Tell him to sharpen his spear and pray to Aphrodite that she may again favor us with a great victory. Me, I shall rouse the Amazons and say to them that the time is at hand for them to show forth their mighty prowess in behalf of Troy."

Though Helen possessed the face and figure that had launched a thousand Achaean ships she was not entirely confident in her matchless beauty, and she was well aware of the Amazonian warriors of Thermoden who had joined them in the city of Troy. They were giants like the wood hewers from the hills, but there was not a man among them, and many of them were beauties of awesome strength and proportion, so Helen had taken care to keep Paris isolated and occupied with her amorous attentions, so that his mind did not wander and temptation did not readily present itself in Amazonian form.

Now, Helen returned through the wide corridors of King Priam's castle, diaphanous dress streaming behind her as she passed through ivory arches and luxuriant tapestries that rustled with chill drafts. Within the wing of the castle reserved to them, she found her husband lounging upon a divan and plucking at a harp.

Helen rushed to him and kissed him with fervent passion, upsetting the harp so that it crashed to the floor in a great cacophony of vibrating strings.

When finally he could take a breath Paris asked, "Does this mean you've forgiven me for thoughtlessly dying and leaving you to the ministrations of my brother?"

"I shall never forgive you for that," sighted Helen. "Unless perhaps you agree never to die again."

Paris thrust his hands around Helen's waist and held her on his lap. "Is there some danger rearing up to devour me?"

"Your father worries that the Achaeans are again growing bold enough to come to battle. Their wine is making them brave."

"I had hoped they would tear down their ship walls and float for home once the harsh storms of winter died," said Paris. "Achilles is slain. How many other of their heroes must die before they think better of their ill-planned war?"

"Menelaus must die before their will is broken," said Helen, "and would that I could administer the killing thrust myself."

"Leave that to me," said Paris.

Helen caressed his cheek. "Oh, no, Paris, do not attempt such a thing. You are a mighty lover, but few can match Menelaus's fierce might in battle. Already you have turned away from his wrath. Smite him down with arrow or spear, but do not venture within distance of his sword—for he has slain many men of strength and valor. And watch for Neoptolemus, lest he possess the prowess of his father in battle. He will be hot for vengeance against the man who slew his father."

"Neoptolemus?" questioned Paris. "I know him not."

"He is the stripling son of Achilles, come recently to the battle on the Far Traveler whose captain is Diomedes."

"Need I fear a stripling?" questioned Paris. "Is it possible that he has not yet inherited the might of Achilles?"

"If not the might, then perhaps the haughtiness," replied Helen, "for he struts about the field as if he is the master of all he surveys."

"I see you have been spying upon the enemy again, but in the meantime my thoughts have been upon nothing but love."

Helen laid a lingering kiss upon her husband's lips. "So is it me you think of or have you composed a sonnet to the uncouth Amazonian beauties who fill fair Troy with their bawdy jests and coarse conduct?"

"Why," replied Paris with a sly grin, "I scarcely have desire to consider another besides my wife, whose loveliness surpasses all Amazonian beauty."

"And also the beauty of nymphs of sea or land?"

"That was never in question," said Paris, who found amusement in her jealousy. "Do I have time to sing you a song of my love or should I immediately gird myself for battle?"

"I think there is time enough for love and for songs of love," said Helen.

†††

When finally the battle was arrayed, Paris went down in his chariot to defend against the vast forces of the Achaeans who finally left behind their hovels tacked together from the hulls of scuttled ships, and came marching up the slopes, sunlight gleaming from a forest of spears. Their fierce faces were helmed, and they bore shields before them to arrest the spear and arrows of the Trojans.

Paris's father, King Priam, rode in a chariot alongside, and the cruel-eyed Deiphobus in a chariot on his other flank. Priam's horses were caparisoned in golden armor that gleamed back the sunlight. His own armor was fashioned in brass polished to a blinding glow, and a pair of red-plumed Amazons, twin daughters of Penthesileia and granddaughters of the war god Ares, Oywen and Demetra, served him as shield bearers.

They were said to be comely women, but now their faces were covered with violet-painted visors that completely concealed their features, but for their piercing eyes of the purest blue. Golden hair spilled from beneath these helms and the ends were plaited with strange ornamentations that

Paris's father, King Priam, rode in a chariot alongside...

included the knucklebones of slain enemies. These warriors were broad-hipped and wide-shouldered and bore sword and shield.

The shield bearers of Paris and Deiphobus were not so striking, but they were fierce men tried and proven in the many battles against the Achaeans.

"Are you ready, brother?" asked Deiphobus as they descended toward the oncoming Achaean ranks. "Is your courage strong or do you plan to flee again before the wrath of Menelaus, with whose wife you have taken your liberties time and again?"

"As have you," replied Paris with an icy rejoinder, reminding Deiphobus that while Paris had languished in the protection of Aphrodite, he had stolen away Helen.

"My weeks with her were scarcely enough to satisfy," said Deiphobus. "And surely you did not expect a woman like Helen to go unclaimed for long?"

"But you claimed her the day after my presumed death—with no sign of my body," replied Paris.

"It was not only I who presumed Menelaus had smitten you with such fierceness that your body had been turned to dust or presumed that Menelaus had carried you away to nail your corpse to the Achaean ship walls. We found your crumpled armor and aught else."

"Nay," replied Paris. "It was Aphrodite who carried me away from Menelaus's wrath, and she appeared to me in a dream, in the guise of Helen, so I thought I was in our bedchamber."

"It must be nice," replied Deiphobus, without bothering to disguise his jealousy, "to be the pet of a goddess who will snatch you from harm's grasp and then mask herself in the form of your wife so that she may give you pleasure. Would that all of us poor Trojans were so unfortunate as you."

"And you took advantage of my absence to force yourself upon my wife, brother!" he spat the last with an evident distaste.

"My condolences, dear brother!" replied Deiphobus, "but I have difficulty finding sorrow in my heart for one who spent his time away in the embrace of a goddess—and Helen seemed to enjoy my attentions well enough."

Now, King Priam became aware of the squabble between his progeny. "Silence, the both of you! Turn your attentions to the battle ahead lest your concentration be so divided that an Achaean spear smite the one or the both of you to the earth, and I am forced to grieve the loss of even more of my sons!"

Truly it had gone hard on King Priam, for he had been nigh on inconsolable since Achilles had slain both the mighty Hector and his young son Troilus. To make matters worse Helenus had disappeared from the city, amidst his anger and jealousy when Deiphobus had seized Helen, after Paris was presumed dead.

As Priam warned, the attack came quickly. Several charioteers breaking from the Achaean front and driving toward a gap in the Trojan lines where some shield bearers had stumbled and left an opening. This gap moved to close, but not before the mighty Odysseus of the Achaeans rode his chariot into the shield wall, hit hard, and was catapulted over the defending lines and into the midst of the Trojans.

He was followed hard by Diomedes through the gap he had broken in the shield wall, and then the stripling warrior, Neoptolemus, who was so much in the mold of his father that he appeared to be the very likeness of Achilles striding through the chaos, smiting down Achaean with swift spear and lightning sword, wherever he strode.

Another warrior came new to the battlefield; some said he was Philoctetes, son of King Poeas of the far island Meliboaea, and famed archer. Indeed, he demonstrated his prowess by shooting from the very seat of his chariot while it ranged back and forth between the enemy lines before the mass of them joined in battle, and he was targeting no ordinary soldiers, for he bent his bow and sent his arrows arching across the Trojan's battle array and in the direction of the sons of nobility.

Paris cursed as an arrow sliced across his calf. "Not even I can shoot so far! How did he strike me thus?"

"I fear," replied King Priam as he steered his horses and chariot toward the flank where an enterprising contingent of Achaeans assayed to break through the wing before it could close, "that the dire prophecies have come true and that the bow and the arrows of Heracles have found their way to the field of battle! Was not Philoctetes known to have been gifted the bow by Heracles himself?"

"But Philoctetes is said to be a cripple with a wounded leg," cried Paris.

"Does he appear to be crippled to you?" questioned Priam from between his fierce Amazonian guards who lifted their shields, red plumes streaming, as his chariot charged into the fray. "Have your shield bearers serve you well, lest I lose another son!"

They broke apart as Priam's chariot rounded the battle lines in search of Achaean heroes that the king and his Amazons might smite. Then, just before the arrayed warriors melted into shambolic fury and horrible bloodshed, Philoctetes ranged another arrow, which the unprepared shield bearers of Paris failed to stop. The arrow slipped between their shields and struck Paris in the shoulder, so that he reeled back and nearly slipped from his chariot.

One of his shield bearers reached out and caught Paris so he did not fall, but perhaps it had been better if he let the princeling slide out the back, for when he grasped Paris's arm, he let down his shield, and another arrow smote Paris's brass breast plate, the point striking through and between his ribs.

Now, Philoctetes chariot ranged far away, and it seemed they had nothing more to fear from Heracles' bow, but as Paris reeled from the pain, a third arrow, shot into the blinding rays of the sun, and then descending from above, slipped past the upraised shield of the second bearer, and caught Paris below the helm, the point driving into his left eye, destroying his sight, and pushing dangerously near his brain.

Paris fell to the floor of his chariot with a groan. One of his shield bearers lifted a brass target overhead, lest yet another arrow fall, while the driver of the chariot turned it back toward the gates of Troy, drove it beneath the portcullis, and wildly through the city streets, where the women and children cried out in alarm at the sight of Prince Paris's chariot fleeing the fray.

They drove at a reckless pace, calling to the guards at the palace gates, so that they were opened up to usher the mortally wounded Paris inside. Helen, from the walls of Troy, had seen the arrows of Heracles rain from the sky, and in horror rushed down, all the while praying Paris's wound weren't as serious as she feared.

She gave a loud and anguished cry when she saw the trio of shafts that protruded from Paris's body. "Oh, my husband, what have they done to you?!"

Paris gave a barely perceptible response, murmured from between his lips, for he feared to move lest the arrow in his eye shift nearer to his brain, and the pain made it difficult for him to form coherent thought, let alone articulate coherent words. "Death is upon me. There is only one who can save me now..."

"Who?" pleaded Helen. "Who can save you from these horrible wounds?!"

"Only the one who I spurned and rejected—the one I tossed away as so much rubbish, when I laid my eyes upon your incomparable beauty."

"Oenone!" cried Helen. "Are you sure that only Oenone can heal your wounds?"

"Ironic, isn't it," gasped Paris, "that the one I deemed as worthless is now the only one who can save my life."

"Tell me it isn't so," replied Helen. "Surely, we can make sacrifice to Aphrodite and she will again find a way to spare you!"

"Nay," said Paris. "She came to me in a dream and told me that Zeus had forbidden her to save me any longer—told me that she could no longer interfere."

"And yet she did, in helping you slay Achilles!" protested Helen, as she watched the blood pooling beneath Paris's helm.

"Go ahead and make sacrifice to Aphrodite," said Paris, "but it is useless. She has been forbidden, and can no longer circumvent the words of Zeus. The heroes of men have been too haughty and he would see them destroyed for their vanity."

"I will," said Helen with resolve. "I will make sacrifice to Aphrodite, and she will find a way to save you for me."

"Then go and do it," said Paris, "but know that they are wasted moments, for not even Aphrodite can move directly against the command of Zeus. If you go to the shrines of Aphrodite, I will surely die."

"But Oenone?" objected Helen, saying the name as if it were the most loathsome word that might ever touch her lips. "You would have me humble myself and go to Oenone?!"

"I would have you do nothing that your heart does not tell you to do," replied Paris with a groan. "But Oenone is the only one with the gift of healing who might spare my life and perhaps even spare the sight of my eye. I have seen her nurse men from the brink of the grave—men with wounds so grievous that their entrails were spilling from their bodies, and yet she brought them to health and vigor because she possesses the healing gifts of her father Cebren."

Helen considered this for long moments, wrestling with her pride and with her vanity, and wrestling with the sacrifice she knew she would have to make in order to save her husband's life. "Very well. I will leave Troy by the back gate and go into the mountains to Oenone's tower, where she has kept her solitude with the son of your first marriage, and I will cast myself upon her mercies. I will beg for your life, whatever be the cost."

"Do not go alone," replied Paris, "lest the Achaeans be roaming behind the city and Menelaus take you as a prize."

"I shall not go alone," lied Helen, but in truth she could not stand for any to see her humbled before Oenone. It would not do for them to witness a woman, whom nations had fought over, whose beauty had launched a thousand ships, humbled to the very dust.

So, even while the battle raged at the front of the city—the Trojans being put to the worst of it—Helen donned a disguise of the rags of the mountain shepherds and slipped through a covert at the back of the city, showing the guard her face, and letting her beauty work its way upon his heart, so that he swiftly gave an oath that he would allow her exit and divulge her passing to no one.

Helen left behind the high walls of Troy, moving quickly through the rough and tortuous paths, and up the rocky and boulder strewn slopes that led up the mountain to the lonely tower where Oenone kept her bitter and solitary vigil. No Achaean patrols molested or detained her and so finally, weary from a long day's travel she mounted the great stone steps that were hewn from the very mountainside and to the base of chalky white monoliths that formed the foundation of the tower.

For a moment, Helen thought she caught sight, from the corners of her sloe eyes, the shadow of a voluptuous figure upon the high crenellations of the spire, but when she cast her gaze directly she saw nothing in the gap between those mute stone teeth. Biting down the ignominious shame of requiring aid from the one whose very home and husband she had usurped, she climbed those high and broad steps to the narrow and low door set in the base of the tower and she lifted a knocker, formed in the aquiline visage of Cebren's face, and let it fall, resounding through the lower tower levels with a musical tone that reminded her of the strings of a harp—but perhaps a hundred of them playing at once, in some celestial harmony.

For a long time she was left to wallow in her own pity upon that doorstep, too proud to lift the knocker a second time and too forlorn to do naught else but sink upon the steps, rest her weary legs and let the tears trace runnels down her dusty cheeks as she considered how her husband hovered near death and how once again she might be forced to the bed of Deiphobus, should Oenone be unable or unwilling to aid Paris.

Finally, after an interminable wait in the tower's shade, eyes stinging and red, she swallowed down her pride and rose on weary bones to lift the knocker again, but ere she could touch it the door slipped open and a young man of unblemished feature and burgeoning handsomeness that might one day rival that of Paris's stood in the opening.

"You are Helen—the usurping wife of my father, who has abandoned me and my mother," stated the young man.

Indeed, Helen recognized the features of Paris in that face. "You are Corythus."

"I am," said the young man. "Do you finally bring me words of reconciliation from my absent father? Does he desire me to come and join at his side in the battle to repel the Achaean hosts?"

"Your father loves you very much and is proud of the fine man you have become," lied Helen, for so enraptured had Paris been in Helen, that scarcely a word he had spoken about Oenone or the son he had sired by her. "But all I bear today is ill tidings. Paris has fallen in battle this very morn and has three Achaean arrows in his body—one in his shoulder, another in his breast, and the third in his left eye."

Corythus appeared unmoved by this news. "Then finally the gods have given him fair compensation for the ill treatment of the wife and son they once blessed him with. I shall pass the news to my mother that we may thank the gods that our prayers have been answered."

Helen's voice came from her lips, strangled and wretched, the musical tones that had enraptured so many men no longer carrying from her throat. "You made entreaty to the gods to bring this fate upon your very own father?!"

"He has been no father to me, since ten years hence he returned to Troy on the Aphrodite with you in his arms. And in truth I not only prayed for his demise, but prayed even more fervently that perhaps he might acknowledge me as his son, seek me out, and beg my forgiveness—but barring that, I would settle for a just compensation for my ill treatment. So when you came to our door, I first hoped it might be you carrying kind words from my father—but now I see it is my second prayer which has been answered."

Now, Helen, seeing how this young man perceived the way in which he had been wronged, went to her knees. "I beg of you—for the love of you that I know your father still harbors in his heart—entreat your mother, Oenone, that she come to Troy and employ her miraculous healing arts so that your father might be saved. There is none other who might have the chance of saving his life!"

A low and husky voice spoke from the shadows behind Corythus and, now, emerged the nymph Oenone, a dark beauty, small in stature, but statuesque in form. Surely, such a loveliness would have satisfied any man who had not gazed upon her own beauty, considered Helen, but she threw such vanities aside and pressed her face into the dust of the doorstep.

"What wants Helen of Sparta, who before had nothing but sneers and condescension for Oenone, the rightful wife of Paris?" said the nymph with quavering words.

Helen spoke from the dust into which her lips were pressed. "Oenone, I cast aside all my pride and beg of you, come to Troy and use your renowned healing arts upon Paris, who lies dying in his bed."

"You do not cast aside all your pride," observed Oenone. "You do not come to me in sack cloth and ash. You do not come to beg my forgiveness for the wrong you have done."

"Nay," admitted Helen, "for what hot-blooded woman could resist the handsome Paris of Troy, come across the wine red deeps and whispering honeyed words of love? I do not seek your forgiveness, because no woman of passion could resist such a man as Paris, and would cast aside every consideration so that they might own him—but I do come to you, throwing aside my pride so that I might beg of you to save his life."

Oenone's long and dark lashes narrowed to slits. "Never have I turned away Achaean or Trojan when they come to my door seeking treatment. Even now, I have fourteen men within these tower walls, who have sought me out that I may heal them from their wounds."

"You are most magnanimous and kind," said Helen.

Oenone, however was not moved by Helen's honeyed words. "Do you know why they came to me, clinging to the last vestiges of their lives and the hopes that I might possess the skills to heal them?"

Helen's lips moved in the dust of the doorstep, though she feared she knew the answer. "Tell me why, Oenone."

"It was because they were wounded in a war which was brought about by the unthinking selfishness of two people, Prince Paris of Troy and Helen of Sparta, who with no thought for the lives of any others, embarked on an affair that has ruined many nations. How many lives have been lost because you and Paris decided that nothing else in all of Greece and Asia mattered, except for the passion you two shared? How selfish can a man and woman be that they will persist in nine years of war and spend countless lives, both noble and common, so they can be together? How many loyal wives have lost husbands and sons to spear and sword because you and Paris could not restrain your lusts? How many?"

"Too many," admitted Helen, who had only recently begun to count the cost and realize the damage of her folly.

"So you say, now," replied Oenone, whose bitterness was not assuaged. "But the battle persists. You do not return to your former husband, nor do you return my husband to me."

"That is what I come to tell you," choked out Helen. "Use your healing arts upon Paris. Save his life! And I will stand aside. You may have him back and I will allow it."

"You will allow it?" questioned Oenone. "You are very magnanimous with another woman's husband. In your pride, you imagine you are the rightful wife of Paris. What of you? Will you return to Menelaus?"

"I cannot return to Menelaus," said Helen. "He has sworn to slay me for my perfidy. Probably, Deiphobus shall lay claim on me, and I shall have to endure his foul touch until the day the gods take my life."

"A fitting punishment," decided Oenone, "but perhaps you protest too much. Deiphobus is a cruel man, but not unhandsome."

"All men are ugly once you have gazed upon the radiance of Paris," said Helen. "Surely, we have this common ground."

"We do," agreed Oenone, "and almost your offer to give me back my husband persuades me to help him."

"Almost?" choked out Helen. "Have I not fully persuaded thee?"

"Just because you have sworn to stand aside does not mean that Paris's heart will be with me," said Oenone. "Always will he dream of you and if you are in the same city, even at the farthest corner of the world he would not be satisfied to leave you, no matter if I saved his life. In truth, you and Paris are a perfect match for each other—both utterly selfish and entirely enraptured with the other, as if you were characters in a play in which no one else mattered."

"I swear to you," cried Helen, "that I will not allow Paris to touch me from this day henceforth, should you save his life!"

"That is not enough," said Oenone. "For as long as Paris lives this war will continue—that I have foreseen. Better to sacrifice his life and to save the life of thousands of others."

Helen, abasing herself even further, crawled across the floor and clutched at Oenone's ankles, her tears bathing her feet. "Please take mercy upon Paris. Do with me, what you will, but please spare Paris's life!"

Oenone looked with cold disdain upon the woman who had stolen away her happiness. "Corythus, please remove this woman from the tower."

Corythus obeyed, prying the wailing Helen from Oenone's ankles and dragging her out onto the broad steps. He closed and barred the heavy door and for many hours Helen beat her fists bloody against those thick panels, crying and wailing, begging and pleading, but Oenone shut her ears against the howling entreaties of Helen—once of Sparta and now of Troy.

"Unwind a rope from the back window and lower yourself out of the tower," Oenone directed her son Corythus. "Go to the Achaeans and tell them that if they hurry, perhaps they may find Helen at the door of our tower or maybe upon the trail back to Troy. If they are able to retrieve Helen, perhaps the Achaeans will take to their ships and return home and this bloodshed and suffering might end."

"I will go swiftly, mother," said Corythus.

Not long after Corythus departed, sobs wracked Oenone's breast and tears of sorrow traced her fair features.

Helen's vigil at the door did not last long enough for the Achaeans to find her unprotected on the trail, for seeing that her pleadings fell upon deaf ears, she returned to Troy so that she might be at the side of her dying husband.

All the luxuries and fineries of royalty could not save Paris's life, and he gave a last convulsive gasp as the point of the clipped arrow slipped deeper and pierced his brain. He clutched at Helen's bloodied hands and died with words of his undying love for Helen upon his trembling lips.

Deiphobus stood nearby, observing his brother's death. "Three days," he told Helen, "I shall let you mourn three days and then I shall come to fetch you and bring you to my home."

From her high tower, Oenone heard the death knells ringing from the temple of Aphrodite, marking the passing of Prince Paris of Troy. She tore her robe and beat her breast in anguish, then descended with wracking sobs, from the tower and to the rear coverts of Troy.

Oenone was known to the city guard who was posted at the rear covert, for she had healed his brother of a grievous spear wound to the chest, and he allowed the forsaken nymph entrance to Troy. She went to the center square where Paris's body was laid upon a funeral pyre, the Trojan troops, arrayed in resplendent armor and bristling phalanxes of spears, around and paying their respects to the man whose impetuous actions had brought death and destruction upon their fair city.

"Light the pyre," cried King Priam, who stood next to his wife Hecuba, whose beauty was undimmed by her great sorrow.

Immediately, torch bearers heeded his command, rushing forward and hurling the flaming brands into the oil-soaked pyre. Flame burst high around the corpse of Paris, the beauty of his legendary visage turned to ash in but a few instants of the all consuming flame.

"And let those who failed to defend him join Paris in death as well," continued King Priam.

Paris's shield bearers were bound hand and foot, and Trojan soldiers slit their throats, dragged their twitching bodies forward and hurled them into the flames.

Then cried the husky and anguished voice of Oenone who had worked her way through the crowds so she might observe the funerary rites of her once husband. "Then let me die also! For I failed to defend Paris, failed to give him succor when his life was in my hands!"

So saying, Oenone burst from the crowds, black hair streaming and hurled herself onto the pyre where she gathered the burning body of Paris in her arms, and died with horrible shrieks that echoed to the ears of her father, the river god, Cebren, who from that day turned his favor away from the Trojans that they might suffer, one day soon, the same fate as his daughter.

THE END

BACK TO A FAMILIAR WORLD

This is the third story in a cycle of Trojan War tales which I have written, the first two having been published in *Pulpology* and *Weird Worlds of Joel Jenkins* 2 and 3. One might think that I have great hubris and temerity to retell these tales and perhaps I have no business doing so—but I justify myself by having chosen to relate a number of stories which have been pieced together from disparate legends.

For example, Homer's *Iliad* is but a fragmentary telling of the Trojan War and does not include the story of the Trojan horse and the fall of Troy. That part of the story comes from Virgil's Aeneid. The story I have just told, No Wrath Like a Nymph Scorned, is derived from various sources such as the *Bibliotheke* by Psuedo-Apollodorus, Homer's Iliad, and the Quintus Smyrnaeus, among others. Though a complete tale, in and of itself, it is obviously just a portion of the vast tapestry of stories that make up the legends surrounding the Trojan War.

Though Paris is a most selfish of protagonists, his story is important because his actions caused the entire Trojan War and brought about the deaths and suffering of thousands. The legend of Paris and Helen is one where love did not conquer all and, instead of being triumphant, destroyed a nation.

JOEL JENKINS - inhabits the heron-haunted reaches of the Pacific Northwest where tales of Sasquatch and ghosts may be more fact than legend. For a current listing of published books visit JoelJenkins.net.

The City in the Clouds

BY
BARBARA DORAN

Sun Wukong took the register, crossed out all the names in the monkey section, and threw it on the floor with the words, "The account's closed. That's an end of it. We won't come under your control any longer."
— Journey to the West (attributed to Wu Cheng'en)

The judge slammed the table so hard it set the wings of his cap fluttering behind his head. Accustomed to the noise, and their judge's temper, his guards gazed sternly ahead of them. The young man kneeling before him, on the other hand, nearly jumped out of his skin.

He was a skinny bit of nothing, was Weijing. Broad cheekbones, narrow jaw, thick brows and more dirt and stink on him than a pig in its sty. His clothes—rags more like—were equally filthy bits of patchwork. His shoulder-length shaggy dark hair hadn't been groomed in weeks and his left eye was swollen black and blue from a guard's fist.

To prove he'd earned the blow, Weijing said, "You're going to break your mallet if you keep doing that."

Judge Li tightened his grip but controlled his urge to slam the lacquered wood bar down again. "I asked you for the reading of your name, you ignorant little boy!" They needed it for the court records; use the wrong characters and a prisoner might claim mistaken identity later. "Or are you too ignorant to know even that much?"

"I can read, and write a little, but there are so many possibilities." Weijing counted on his fingers. "Unfinished work. Venerable old age. Spirit Essence...."

It took Judge Li a moment to realize the prisoner had freed his hands and now he really did split his mallet. "Can't any of you idiots keep this bastard properly chained?" His men leapt forward, forcing the boy's hands behind his back. "Forgery fits you best, nuisance!"

A voice came from the back of the room. "Might I suggest; Perilous Path?"

The newcomer startled everyone, even the guards. Only Weijing, held down by four big, burly, men, kept his eyes to the floor. Even then he was irrepressible. "I like that one. I'll take it."

Everyone else stared at the slim short fellow standing at the entrance to the judgment hall. He had carefully groomed long black hair, bound in a topknot held back by a delicate gold hairpiece. His robes were plain reddish-brown, trimmed in a delicately embroidered pattern of red and gold. Those knowledgeable of such things would have recognized *Haixi* cloth; a fabric imported from a distant desert land and said to come from a species of water-sheep.

Hard-heeled boots clicked on the floor as the newcomer walked forward; almost, but not quite, swaggering. He carried himself like a warrior, though he wore neither weapon nor armor. He seemed too slight and fragile to be anything but a scholar.

"How dare you enter my court unann...." Judge Li faltered as his eyes met the stranger's. The man's face was young and unlined, but his gaze suggested he'd seen far more than anyone else present. The hermit of Huangshan Peak had such eyes, though this was obviously not him. For one thing, the hermit's eyes were a true black and this man's were an unusual light hazel shade. "Who are you?"

"Mei Youren." The man grinned, revealing slightly jagged teeth. "Write it how you wish. I've come for the prisoner." Before Judge Li could object, Mei held up the gold enameled seal of an officer of the Imperial Court. Before anyone could rise and bow properly, he added, "I'd rather not stand on ceremony. I'm in something of a rush and require the boy now, if you please."

The request puzzled Judge Li. "Why in the world would you want a petty thief and swindler? Or why does the Court want him, rather?"

"He's the one who claimed to have visited the floating city of Huanjing, yes?"

Claimed was the operative word. "He is. But he's a liar. He's been trouble here in Huangshan City for years." Judge Li smacked the table to emphasize the list. "Broke into the hermitage and tried to steal Hermit Guchang's secrets. Performed a vulgar dance for the Hermit's students. Started a fight with a gang over a broken down hovel in the beggar's district. Stole weapons from the armory. Broke into Lord Guang's house, broke the central pillar and extorted a suit of armor. And to top it all off, he was caught trying to get into my records to burn everything to do with his crimes."

Officer Mei whistled and Judge Li wished there wasn't quite so much admiration in the man's expression. The last thing young Weijing needed was encouragement. "A most desperate and despicable character indeed." The man stepped past the guards and lifted Weijing to his feet by his chin. "What of your visit to the floating city? Is it all a pack of lies as Judge Li says? Have you really been there?"

"Honored One, how could I dare lie to someone as big and strong and handsome as yourself? Not only have I visited Huanjing, I was born there."

Judge Li slammed his mallet down again, but Officer Mei waved off the interruption. Gently he turned the boy's face and gazed sharply into the young man's eyes. "I am sure truth and your august self are but passing acquaintances, but exert yourself for your own sake."

"I... I was born there. Truly."

"The whole thing's nothing but a story, Honored One." Judge Li faltered as the officer raised his free hand for silence. Li quieted, though he yearned to continue his explanation. The so-called floating city of Huanjing appeared over Huangshan peak when conditions were right but all it was was a mirage, a reflection of Huangshan City itself. Even its name—mirage capitol—proved that much. There were no fairies, no golden godlings; just shadows and dreams reflected in the mist.

The officer examined the boy's eyes for a long moment and Judge Li was surprised to see real fear in Weijing's expression. Then, with a laugh, Mei said. "Good. Good. Do you know when it's due to appear next?"

"It comes and goes as it wills, sir. I've no idea."

"You at least know how to get to it?"

"I... no. I left it years ago. I don't know how to go back. I never wanted to. You don't want to visit.... It's... not what you think it is."

Another laugh. "Child, you have no idea what I think it is." Mei set the boy down on his feet and for the first time Judge Li realized he'd been holding Weijing several inches above the ground. "Very well. Judge Li, release this boy into my custody. Even if he knows no way back to his birthplace, he knows its streets. He will assist me."

"You can't possibly trust him."

"I trust him as far as I can throw a stone from Nu Kua's wall. Which is to say, not particularly far at all. Nonetheless, write the release form and I will be responsible—Gods help me—for him."

With assurances such as that, and having no real desire to deal with the brat any more than he had to, Judge Li took brush in hand and wrote the order.

It wasn't until much later, when he actually looked at Mei's chop—the red-ink stamp from his imperial seal—that Judge Li realized the characters for the officer's name could be read in an entirely different way.

Meiyou Ren. Nobody.

Trailing behind Officer Mei, Weijing watched for a chance to make a break for it. It wasn't just a general dislike for doing what he was told. Nor even his dislike of the law and all those associated with it. It wasn't even the fact that Officer Mei scared him straight down to the bones.

No, what he really wanted to avoid was their destination. He'd done all he could to forget the misty land of his birth. Had managed to persuade himself that he belonged to this solid reality. Had managed to—mostly—bury the nightmares. To go back was to remember things he never wanted to see again.

"Don't think I can't follow you wherever you go." Mei's voice was quiet, but its tone sent a chill through Weijing. "You'd be surprised just how far I can pursue you."

A herd of oxen interrupted them, running through the street and trampling everyone in their path. Street carts fell over, scattering produce and other goods everywhere and the sound of shouts and screams filled the air. Seeing his chance, Weijing dodged sideways, ducked beneath one cart and slipped through a cracked door, not bothering to open it as he passed. "Tried to steal secrets," he muttered to himself derisively. "Say rather successfully stole 'em.... YIPE!"

The hand that caught Weijing by the wrist and forced him to one knee was the same amazingly strong one that had lifted him by the chin not an hour past. "You don't listen well; do you, mist-walker?"

Weijing slipped sideways, letting his body become as mist again, then streamed outside. Behind him, he heard Mei telling someone, "Don't worry, ma'am. Here. A gold tael for your pains."

Then the officer was in front of Weijing, stepping forward out of thin air so fast the boy barely changed directions in time. Under any other circumstance, Weijing would have applauded, might even have offered some smart remark on the subject. Right now all he wanted was escape.

They moved through the crowd, Weijing shifting to mist and exhausting his stolen magic with terrified profligacy. Officer Mei never broke a sweat, simply stepping out of nowhere to appear in just the right position to force Weijing off in another direction. It took several such encounters before

Weijing—usually cleverer than this—realized he was being herded. Until, at last, he found himself shifting right into someone's bath.

Most water didn't give Weijing a moment's difficulty. Hot, steaming, soap-filled water on the other hand, was a problem. The steam interacted with his mist form strangely, so when he shifted back to solidity, he was coughing and wheezing and entirely oblivious to the brothel's 'ladies' beating him over the head with whatever came to hand.

The only thing Weijing did notice was the strong hand picking him up by the nape of the neck and dragging him out of the water. "Ladies, my deepest apologies. My child has no manners. Isn't that right, child?" The hand made Weijing's head bob in agreement and he was sure he'd be sick. "If one of you would fetch the proprietress so I might make reparations? Not to mention purchase the use of a room for the two of us? Preferably one with a private bath."

"I'll go." A youngster just about Weijing's seventeen years went running outside.

"I'll need clothes for this young miscreant as well," Mei called after her. "And food. It looks to me like he hasn't eaten for a while."

The room was arranged by the time Weijing was done coughing and choking. Dragged inside, helpless and confused, he was dumped into a bathtub. Steaming hot water poured down on him and he knew he couldn't escape again. Then he felt his shirt and trousers being ripped off his body.

"Hey! Don't!"

"Your choice, Weijing. Either I wash you, or you wash yourself. You stink worse than the Jade Emperor's stables."

Though he yearned to ask how Officer Mei could know what the Emperor of Heaven's stables smelled like, Weijing grabbed the cleaning towel and began scrubbing himself until the water turned black from his filth. "I'll find a way to escape later, you know."

"I know. And I'll hunt you down. I require your knowledge of the City of Ghosts, boy. There's nothing you can do to escape me." By this time Officer Mei was seated at the table, sipping delicately from a porcelain cup of tea. He gazed out the window. "Though you're welcome to try. As many times as you like."

Feeling a chill in his bones, Weijing decided not to argue the point. "You're a sorcerer. I didn't know the court employed sorcerers."

"There's a great deal you don't know. Including how to keep yourself to yourself when you mist-walk. You're lucky you didn't drown back there. How many transformations did you steal from the Hermit? All seventy-two?"

"Strictly speaking, I don't think you can steal knowledge. Just study it without permission." The Hermit had ways to control his former slave, but most of the spells he'd used to do so had been easily learned. Mist-walking had taken more subterfuge but by then Weijing had gotten quite good at evading the old man. Good enough to escape him, certainly. Weijing shuddered. That was another place he didn't want to think about.

"Still, did you learn all seventy-two or not?"

"Not." Weijing had focused on mist-walking, knowing it was the only way he could escape his former master. And as soon as he had learned it, he'd run. Guchang hadn't followed, though Weijing couldn't guess why. "Enough to get by."

"We'll have to hope so," Mei muttered. "Especially where we're going."

As Weijing climbed out of the bath and dried himself, the officer pointed at the big bowl of vegetarian soup someone had brought in earlier. "Eat up. It looks like you haven't been properly fed for months. Years even. I hope you don't mind the lack of meat. I stopped eating it years back."

Weijing avoided meat himself, though for different reasons than most people. He didn't comment, just took the bowl and started sucking down its contents as fast as he could. Only when he'd finished did he notice Mei watching him with an odd, thoughtful, air. "What?"

"Tell me, all those crimes you committed. Why?"

Ordinarily, Weijing would have evaded the question, but Mei's eyes held only curiosity. "I 'stole' Guchang's secrets to get away from him. I started that fight in the beggars' quarter because the big beggars were picking on some kids, the same kids I stole weapons from the armory for. Same with Lord Guang. And I was just clearing the record so the police would leave my friends alone."

"And nothing for yourself? Your little games could have gotten you killed a dozen times over."

Weijing shrugged. "I'm not afraid of dying."

The officer shook his head, amused by Weijing's apparent bravado. "I see." He stretched, yawning, and pointed at the bedding laid out on the floor for Weijing. "Sleep. We'll need to leave for the mountain as soon as it's daylight. I hope you haven't made a complete enemy of Guchang. I'm going to need his help before this is over."

Before Weijing could so much as open his mouth to object, Mei went to the bed, curled up and began snoring. Weijing was out of the brothel and back on the streets within minutes. He might have cooperated, might even have tried to find some way to benefit from this madman's mad plans.

But that was before he knew they'd be going to Guchang first. There were few things he feared, but the Hermit of Huangshan peak was first among them.

✝✝✝

It was early morning when Weijing woke to the most wonderful smell in the world. Congee, cooked in a hot broth of some unknown vegetables. Fried bread. Salt eggs. And the familiar too-sweet odor of fresh-picked peaches.

The last scent startled Weijing to full consciousness. It was just past the first days of spring and peaches, fresh peaches, ought to be impossible. There were only two places he'd come across such a thing and neither were places he wanted to be again.

Weijing had holed up an old shrine outside the city, hoping to evade Officer Mei. He should have known better, given the man's sorcery. Reluctantly, he climbed down from the shrine idol's lap and found Mei sitting in front of a small fire, gazing out the door of the shrine.

"I agree. Staying at the brothel would have been complicated. This is better, and quieter." The officer beckoned Weijing forward and something made him obey. He rationalized his cooperation. This man was dangerously persistent. Weijing didn't want to go where Officer Mei led, but he could tell the man was the sort to never let go of an idea once he'd had it. Weijing would have to wait for a better, safer, moment to escape.

Stepping into the courtyard, Weijing paused to look around; breathing the spring air like it was wine. Just beyond the broken gate a broad, gentle, river flowed past, glittering in the sunlight. Willow trees leaned over the water, their branches swirling in the current. Reeds bent in a light breeze and dragonflies swooped and dodged through the grass. The vines covering the shrine's ruined walls rustled, and somewhere a bird sang fit to break the heart.

"The Human World is far too beautiful," Weijing told Mei, accepting the bowl the man offered him with a bow of thanks. "Why in the nine hells would you want to go to the floating city?"

"Huanjing is beautiful too," Officer Mei answered, gazing off distantly at a current in the water whose movement reminded Weijing of a hunting snake. "You were born there. Why don't you like it?"

The answer was one Weijing couldn't give. Not without remembering what he'd long since chosen to forget. "It wasn't for me."

"Did they abuse you? Were you a slave? A child of its streets as you are here in this world?"

None of those things. All of them. Weijing didn't want to think about it and didn't want to remember. "I don't have an answer for you."

Officer Mei handed him a peach. "You will when the time comes," he remarked.

Ignoring Mei's arrogant certainty, Weijing handed the fruit back. "I don't like peaches." He sat down with the bowl. "I ate too many once, years ago. Made me sick."

Taking no offense, Mei bit into the peach himself, the juices, rich and surprisingly golden, dripping down his chin. "Youngsters like you have no self-discipline. It's to be expected, though. One doesn't reach old age and wisdom without going through youth and stupidity first." He grinned at a joke only he understood. "Never mind. Eat your congee. I want to reach the hermitage before nightfall."

Weijing argued against visiting Guchang all the way. It didn't help that every attempt to explain why left him coughing and wheezing. At last he contented himself with the only advice allowed him. "Just don't let your guard down. You'll be fine as long as you pay attention."

"Oh, trust me. I do know that much." Mei juggled a few rocks as he walked behind Weijing, his light eyes glancing around the trail with obvious interest. If Weijing didn't know what he knew, he'd have appreciated the view a great deal more. Pines and beeches covered the steep hillside, as well a few maples. The only path wended its way upwards, switching back and forth as it climbed the cliff towards the peak. There were other, taller mountains in Huangshan, but Guchang had always said he liked this one best. He certainly never left it.

"Now, now. There'll be plenty of time for gawking when we get there." Mei nudged Weijing forward, his hand light on Weijing's shoulder. "This is going to take a while and I've a feeling there's trouble ahead. I'd rather not sit here waiting for it."

Officer Mei's predictions turned out unsurprisingly true. Everyone knew the only way up to Guchang's hermitage was narrow, precarious and not for the faint of heart. It was the hermit's first, unofficial, test of those who sought him. If nothing else, a student of Guchang's had to have a head for heights.

As for the officer's expectation of trouble, it was well known amongst highwaymen that the best pickings came from the sort of high-minded innocent scholars who sought men like Guchang for enlightenment. The rumor that Guchang had the secret of immortality drew would-be sages to him like ants to a pot of honey. And that, in turn, drew bandits.

Weijing was neither bandit nor disciple. The former because he had a peculiar dislike for bloodshed, the latter because Guchang thought him useless. Indeed, from the moment he'd fallen into Guchang's lap as a small child, the old man had made his opinion all too clear. Weijing was an empty-headed nitwit, good for nothing more than fetching and cleaning. And other things. Things that'd driven Weijing to learn the man's magic and escape.

Those skills, stolen or simply illicitly learned, came in handy when the bandits roared down the mountain path. Weijing might not have learned all seventy-two transformations, but he'd learned enough to get him out of the path of a slashing blade. By the time it reached him he was several feet shorter, covered in red and white fur, with a bushy tail and flaps spread between his arms and legs. Before the bandit could react, he'd leapt off the trail, gliding down to land in the treetops several dozen feet below.

As the branches swayed and swung beneath Weijing, he screeched and howled mockingly, clinging tight to his perch. He felt no compunction over leaving Mei to deal with their attackers. If the officer was as good as he seemed, a score of bandits should be no problem. And if he wasn't, well then Weijing was free to go his own way.

The fight was complicated by the terrain. There simply wasn't enough room on the narrow path to allow more than one or two bandits to reach their target. Whereas Mei was fast and light on his feet, seeming to almost float backwards out of their way. Then, without warning, he'd catch hold of an outstretched hand, or an axe's haft, to send its owner tumbling down the steep hill below.

Weijing watched, unsure who to root for. On one hand, he didn't want to be dragged back to Guchang. On the other, he'd been beaten up by those very bandits often enough that he really didn't like the thought of them winning again. Then his own mouth betrayed him and he found himself screeching a warning when an archer towards the back of the fight raised her bow. The arrow's tip glinted with something black and wet; poison, Weijing was sure.

The cry wasn't loud and it wasn't at all coherent. Weijing had not yet learned to speak as a human would when he was transformed. Yet it was

Weijing leapt off the trail, gliding down to land in the treetops below.

enough to catch Mei's attention. The officer looked up the trail, seeming to understand Weijing's non-words as if he'd spoken. Suddenly Mei was gone, only to reappear a moment later right behind the archer. She spun round as he tapped her on the shoulder, then fell when he punched her in the jaw.

"I don't hit children or people smaller than me," Officer Mei remarked to the other bandits as they turned towards him. "But there aren't very many adults who qualify as smaller. Might I suggest that, if you don't want to find out what else I can do, you take your leave? A skilled thief recognizes when the risk outweighs the take, you know."

Neither the suggestion, nor the fact that their opponent was a powerful sorcerer, had the desired effect. Of course, Weijing could have told Mei that this gang had no more sense than a firefly making love to an incense stick. They turned, rushing up the trail at the man as fast as they could.

With a sigh, Mei gestured at the hillside above the trail. "I wonder," he said, as something groaned within the rocks, "Are you any good at riding the avalanche?" Pebbles rained down, a few at first, but rapidly increasing in number, until there seemed to be thousands to millions of the rocks rolling down towards them in a rising cloud of dust.

That had the desired effect and screaming with terror, the bandits raced down the trail, the avalanche following behind. Weijing watched it, turning slowly as the rocks flowed after them. A true rockslide would have cascaded straight down. Even if it'd followed the trail, it would have come to the switchback and gone over. This one followed the bandits like a serpent hunting a mouse.

Something caught Weijing by the nape of the neck and carried him through the air to hang in front of Mei. "Well, aren't you just the cutest thing. What are you? A squirrel? Why not something faster and stronger, like a monkey?"

"I don't like monkeys," Weijing countered, returning to his human form. "They all pick on me. I'm not part of their tribe." He could have bit his tongue at the admission. It hit too close to the heart.

An interested look crossed Mei's face and he seemed about to ask questions. Before he could, however, a quavering old voice called down. "Who is it making such a racket?" The tone changed to irritation. "Oh. It's you, you nuisance brat. Come to beg my forgiveness and crawl back into my service?"

It was Hermit Guchang and from his expression as he peered over the edge of the cliff at them, he was about to send another avalanche down the hillside. Only this one would be aimed at Officer Mei and Weijing.

†††

"You realize it's only because he's under your control that I'm letting that ruffian of yours in."

Under any other circumstance, Weijing would have been disastrously tempted to show his 'keeper' exactly why Guchang didn't trust him. As it was, he couldn't help muttering, "I'm not 'his' ruffian."

"You're my charge until this business is over, boy," Mei told him in a distracted way. The officer was looking at Guchang's servants, the hooded and robed figures who were silently cleaning the hermitage's courtyard. Then he shook himself. "Hush your foolish mouth before you wind up hung upside-down by your heels over the cookpot."

Mei's order made Weijing start. Not just because he feared the threat but because that'd been exactly what Guchang had done to him when he'd been small. Admittedly, he'd spilled all the ink and ruined the calculations Guchang had been poring over, but still, that was hardly a good enough reason to threaten to cook him. Weijing still remembered the terror of that moment.

Returning his attention to the hermit, Mei sipped from his cup. It was excellent tea; of a sort only available in the richest and noblest of houses. A gift—acquisition, rather—from one of the man's students, no doubt. "Well, never mind all that, Hermit Guchang. I haven't come here to discuss the boy... except, of course, where he fits in with my plans."

Guchang spread his hands with a curious expression. "You interest me, Officer Mei. You don't appear to be a seeker of knowledge." He indicated the pathway down the mountainside, adding, "Indeed, you seem to know a good deal already. I've seldom seen such an effective illusion."

"Oh, there's always room for improving one's mind." Mei waved off the compliment. "But it's true I'm not here to become your disciple. I'd rather not be involved with what you do here."

The way Mei spoke was almost abruptly rude and Weijing saw a flash of irritation in Guchang's eyes. It was an expression he knew well and he wondered if he should warn the officer not to push his luck. But, then, if Mei managed to irritate the hermit enough, he might throw them both off the mountain. A better ending, certainly, than other options.

The two men eyed each other and to Weijing's surprise, it was Guchang who looked down. "What is it you're looking for, then?"

"The City in the Clouds. Huanjing."

Guchang raised his eyes again and this time there was a flash of fear. "You can't possibly believe the boy's story. He's just a nuisance wanderer with no family."

As always, the statement set a hollow feeling in Weijing's stomach. No one in any world—this, or the one he'd come from—wanted him. He might as well have sprung, full-grown, from a rock. As loneliness tried to overwhelm him, Officer Mei snorted. "Nonsense, Hermit Guchang. Everyone has family. Admittedly, sometimes one has to look far afield to find them. I, for instance, have brothers and sisters all over the place. Some may even be on this very peak."

Waving off the statement, Guchang continued, "Oh, I'm sure he has parents, somewhere. But just because he landed in my lap out of the sky doesn't mean he came from the City in the Clouds."

"If not, I have no hope of getting there." Officer Mei patted Weijing's shoulder in a way that was almost comforting. Or would be if Weijing trusted anyone's claim to sympathy. "I'm sure you know Huanjing guards its privacy carefully. I can, as you might guess, fly, but not there. Only a child born of their world has a hope of helping me and even that will require subtlety. Not to mention careful timing. I do hope you have some way of divining when the city makes an appearance?"

Hermit Guchang sat silent for the longest moment. "I have studied its comings and goings," he admitted. "I will attempt to discern its next appearance, seeing as how you are an officer of the court. But it may be some time. May I offer you a place to rest? I'm sure you and the boy are tired after your long climb."

It really wasn't all that late and Weijing yearned to speak, to warn his companion of the danger. Except Officer Mei yawned suddenly and looked terribly surprised. "Oh dear. You're right. I really am most amazingly... slee...py." He was out before his head hit the table.

Dourly, Hermit Guchang turned a sharp gaze on Weijing. "Don't just sit there, boy. You know what to do." When Weijing hesitated, the old man snarled, "You escaped me once. Don't think you'll escape again. There are ways of blocking a mist-walker, you know."

Grimly, knowing he hadn't the magic to get him out of this trap a second time, Weijing bowed his head.

"And don't forget to strip him. Bring his things to me when you're done. I want to know who he is and what he's really up to here."

Unable to disobey, Weijing carried the officer off and wondered if he should slit the man's throat before he woke. It'd be kinder really and Weijing didn't know why he hesitated. After all, dead men didn't care when they were gutted and boiled for stew.

And Weijing hated listening to them scream.

†††

Guchang's students were—as always—oblivious to the servant dragging a body through their meditation yard. Weijing didn't know how Guchang kept the young men and women ignorant—illusions, no doubt—but at least it meant he needn't take the long way round to get the officer to the kitchen. The chef—if one could call the horse-faced old nag a chef—wouldn't rouse before sunset. Not that it mattered much. Weijing had never seen one of Guchang's victims waken in time to save themselves.

Convinced of the futility of saving Mei and knowing he'd nowhere to run, Weijing dumped the officer on the bloodied butcher table and surveyed him ruefully. "I tried to warn you," he said. "Let the Gods witness me. I did try." It wasn't his fault he couldn't break Guchang's geas on him. He couldn't do anything to warn a victim of their fate.

"Well, so you did," Officer Mei agreed, hand lashing out so fast Weijing couldn't evade it. "The question is, how deeply are you involved in the Hermit's nonsense?" His fingers grasped Weijing's throat, not quite painfully but tight enough.

Weijing squeaked like a terrified rodent. "You're awake? How are you awake? You can't be awake! The stuff the Hermit uses could knock out an elephant!"

Swinging his feet around to sit up, Mei cocked his head curiously. "An elephant? You sound terribly sure. What earthly reason would Guchang have for sedating an elephant?"

"H... h... his... chef... wanted to... try... a new.. recipe."

"With a whole elephant?" The officer stopped himself. "Never mind. I'm too easily distracted. Answer my question. How deeply involved in this are you?"

"Are... you... going to kill me?"

"I? Kill? Oh, no. I gave up killing years ago. I am, however, going to put you over my knee if you don't answer my question. Tell papa everything, boy. Before I lose my patience."

Weijing wanted to protest that he didn't have a papa and if he did it certainly wasn't Officer Mei. Except he was too scared to argue anymore. "I don't understand the question."

"How many people have you, yourself, killed?"

"I didn't. I haven't. I just...." As usual the attempt to say more ended with a fit of coughing. This time, however, Officer Mei peered down Weijing's throat, then suddenly reached into his mouth, catching hold of something that squirmed and twisted and struggled.

Sure he was choking to death, Weijing wailed, his cry echoed by some other, much smaller, voice. Then the pain was gone and he was left, gasping and wheezing, on the floor. Mei examined whatever it was he'd dragged out of Weijing's throat. A tiny figure, little bigger than an ant, it resembled a human except for its clawed fingers and toes. Its hair was a wild mass of spikey black thorns and its body covered in a greasy purple hide.

"That... was that... what is that?"

"Guchang's geas." Mei examined the creature thoughtfully, taking a jar of mustard from the shelf. With a wry smile, he popped the thing inside, ignoring its screech as he closed the lid. "I'm not sure a homunculus like that counts as life, but I'd rather be safe than sorry later. Now, you were saying?"

It took a moment to formulate an answer. "I've never killed anyone. Just handed them over to the chef and buried the remains in the peach orchard." Weijing waved his hand off towards the southern slope of the peak, where Guchang's magical peaches grew.

"The ones you mentioned before?"

There was a disgusted look on Mei's face that Weijing understood completely. Sickened, he denied the suggestion. "No. The ones I ate were back in Huanjing."

That clearly relieved Mei. "Good. I won't have to rehabilitate you for murder, along with everything else. And I may be able to get you off a bit for abetting, given that unpleasant little geas over there." The jar of mustard jerked sideways a little as its occupant took offense. Thoughtfully, the officer moved the jar down to the bottom shelf, sticking it under a heavy brick. "And stay put," he added firmly.

"Rehabilitate? I don't understand."

"I've taken responsibility for you, boy, remember? It's my job to make sure you're a functioning member of society before I let you go. My sins come back to me, I fear." Officer Mei considered Weijing thoughtfully. "But enough about that. What is old Guchang expecting you to do right now?"

"He wants everything you're wearing."

"That's all?" Officer Mei began stripping. "Though I suppose he wouldn't need you to kill me, given that drug of his."

Feeling like he was being dragged along by an irrepressible and not particularly organized herd of goats, Weijing began folding the man's outer robe. "You knew he was drugging you. Why didn't you do something?"

"To find out what he's going to do. Besides, I still need him to summon Huanjing." Tossing his underclothes to Weijing, the officer snatched up a nearby towel and wrapped it round his waist before Weijing saw more than a glimpse of naked flank. The cloth hung oddly around Mei, but Weijing couldn't work out why it seemed strange. "Now you run along and take my things to Guchang."

"It'll be night soon. You'd better hide, before the chef wakes up."

"I'll handle her. You get moving."

Weijing headed out the door. He was halfway back to Guchang's hut before Mei's comment about Huanjing truly registered. Could Guchang really summon the City in the Clouds? And if so, what did that mean?

"Took you long enough."

"I didn't want to risk damaging anything," Weijing told Guchang as the hermit went through the stack of clothing. "I may be an uneducated lout but I know quality when I touch it."

Guchang's horsehair whisk struck Weijing in the face. "You learned to talk back in your absence. Be silent." Immediately, Weijing obeyed. He couldn't let Guchang know he was free of the geas.

Examining the officer's outer robe, Guchang muttered, "Water-sheep silk. Exquisite stuff, too. I've never seen so much in my life. Linen and cotton. You're right about the quality, at least. I'll have Bull take them to market, once that idiot and his gang find their way back."

Bull was the leader of the bandits they'd met earlier. A bully of the worst sort, he'd gladly attached himself to Guchang's service when he realized the benefits. He and his men protected Guchang's mountain hut from casual visitors and official notice. Only the richest and stupidest of Guchang's would-be disciples could get through, tricked into believing themselves special beyond measure when Bull pretended to be impressed and frightened by their very presence. When they reached Guchang, they were drugged into compliance, sending requests for money and goods until the source dried up. At which point Bull's wife would create a banquet fit for a cannibal king.

Weijing watched the hermit morosely. He yearned for a quiet moment where he could consider Officer Mei's revelations. In the twelve years he'd been Guchang's slave, Weijing had never known the hermit to mention Huanjing except to scoff at those disciples convinced he'd come from there to bring his knowledge to an unworthy world.

A quiet moment was not to be had. Guchang suddenly demanded, "This was all? Are you holding something back?"

Weijing almost answered but remembered he'd been ordered to silence. He wasn't sure if Guchang remembered, but he daren't take the risk. He opened his mouth and began coughing, pretending to choke helplessly under the power of the geas.

"Oh for... speak, boy. Stop that noise and answer me."

Obediently, Weijing said, "This was all he had. His clothes and his seal." The latter sat gleaming on the table, a gold plated block about three inches tall by an inch wide, marked with the officer's rank. Its base contained a red ink pad and a stamp carved with Officer Mei's name.

"There has to be something," Guchang muttered. "A pouch? A weapon?" He went through the robe again while Weijing remembered how Mei had paid for their room. "What is it, boy? You know something? I can see it in your eyes."

Even without the geas, Weijing was unable to defy Guchang's orders. He was just too accustomed to fearful servility here. He pointed to the outer robe. "The sleeve."

"Is no heavier than... well I'll be damned. A pouch?" As Weijing reflected on the accuracy of Guchang's invective, the hermit drew a pouch covered in delicate embroidery out of the robe's flattened sleeve. Gold coins poured from the thing, far more than it ought to have contained.

"Hells," Guchang muttered watching the stream of coins. "I'm going to need something to put this in. Here, boy. You hold this until it's empty. And don't dare take a single coin." The hermit left Weijing standing beside the table to head for his storeroom.

The gold poured out, jingling softly, covering the low table and gleaming in the lamplight. It occurred to Weijing, watching the shining stream that his old master had left himself wide open with his last order.

After all, a handful of gold was not, and never could be, a single coin.

†††

In the end, Weijing left the gold alone. He was a mischief maker, a troublesome nuisance poking his long nose where it wasn't wanted. He wasn't—strictly speaking—a thief. Except when it came to food. Besides, he'd never gotten anything past Guchang before. He feared this time wouldn't be any different.

Weijing was beginning to wonder if he'd end up buried in coins when the flow finally trickled to a halt. Instinctively and without reason to do so, he shook the pouch, as if they didn't have enough coins already. No more gold fell out, but something rattled and he reached in to pull out a rolled up scroll of bamboo slats mounted on red silk cords. Some of the older records in the Magistrate's hall had been stored this way.

Curious, Weijing opened the scroll to find the slats marked with mere nonsense. Long nose. Red ass. Bushy beard. Long arms. He memorized every word, a trick he'd learned from one of Guchang's disciples years ago. Even if he couldn't understand what he'd read immediately, he could go over it in his head later and try to make sense of it.

The sound of something dragging outside made Weijing quickly hide the scroll in his shirt. He straightened himself out just barely in time, for Guchang entered, tugging on a big wooden chest. "Don't just stand there scratching your armpit, boy. Help me put the coins in."

By the time they'd finished it was past dark and Bull and his bandits had returned. The bandit leader was furious with Weijing and only refrained from bashing his skull in again because Guchang ordered the man to leave him alone. "It's my job to punish him. Besides, the man he brought us carried more gold than we've seen in a year. More than sufficient recompense for the trouble he caused you."

"Even so...."

"Even so, take pleasure in knowing the bastard will be joining us for dinner tonight." Guchang sniffed the evening air with a satisfied smirk. "He already smells delicious. Your wife's best work, I think. The old nag has surpassed herself."

The odor of cooking had, indeed, been wafting through the hermitage for almost half an hour. A savory scent, rich, yet delicate, it'd been making Weijing hungry despite his fears. Had Officer Mei fought the chef and lost? Or had old Ma been the loser now forming the main dish of tonight's banquet? Neither was an appetizing thought, yet Weijing couldn't help his mouth watering or his stomach growling.

The meal took less time to serve than usual. Old lady Ma had spells she used to hurry the cooking process. A strange pot that sealed flavor in and another that precisely controlled the temperature. Yet even those tools couldn't hurry perfection, or so she'd been known to say. So it was a surprise when the call to dinner came barely an hour later.

They all gathered in the courtyard, where someone had already prepared the tables beneath the cherry trees, surrounding them with thick wool sitting rugs and decorating them with delicate orchids. Platters of sliced meats, vegetables, and fruits stood ready, though there was no sign of the chef. As for her servants, they were all scurrying around nervously, assisting the diners to their seats and pouring wine into tiny elegant cups.

As always, Weijing felt sorry for the servants, even though they loathed him, throwing filth his way when they thought Guchang wasn't looking, blaming him for their captivity. The big red-haired one had broken Weijing's arm once, in fact. Yet he couldn't blame them for their dislike. He'd been the one who had to keep them in order, back in the day.

Weijing found himself forced to sit on the rug next to Guchang, to both his and the hermit's mutual distaste. Yet something about the whole situation made them fall silent, obediently minding the etiquette of a formal banquet. Even the bandits were behaving properly, following the careful manners of the scholars at the table across from them.

Dish after dish followed and while Weijing usually avoided anything coming from Guchang's kitchen, he found himself unable to do so this time. For one thing, the smell of the food was too tantalizing to ignore. For another, not a single dish he'd taken appeared to be meat. No one else noticed, but he'd borrowed food from the local shrines often enough to recognize particularly fine examples of vegetarian dishes.

The main course was a huge plate of what looked like pork, elegantly sliced, with edges of rich fat. Weijing swallowed at the sight, both entranced by the rich odor and terrified of what it represented. He didn't dare speak, not with the scholars there to hear him. Who was the main course, he wondered, as the servant placed a few delicate slices on his plate.

"Go ahead and eat." Something about the servant's intonation was familiar and Weijing was startled to recognize a pair of hazel eyes looking at him humorously from twisted old features. "Trust me."

"Stop fiddling around." Guchang sounded oddly mellow and Weijing realized the hermit was getting drunk. "I want my share."

As the servant turned away, Weijing hesitated a moment longer before lifting a golden slice to his lips. To his surprise, the 'meat' was nothing of

They all gathered in the courtyard...

the sort. He wasn't sure what it was, exactly, but it was delicious and rich, with an intense flavor he'd never experienced before. He—like the other diners—took to it readily, accepting seconds and thirds.

The final course was a dish of fruit; a mix of pear, peach and lychees. Still mistrusting everything peach, Weijing truthfully claimed he was far too full to eat, allowing Guchang to steal his share. By this time the full moon had nearly reached its zenith, its light brilliant against the blossoms of the trees above them.

As the last dish was placed and the last bit of fruit eaten, Weijing wondered what would happen next. Officer Mei had obviously used sorcery to create this meal and while it'd appeared harmless, Weijing doubted it was as innocent as it seemed. Thus, he wasn't surprised when one of the scholars suddenly started to his feet.

"Wait! I... I remember. You... Guchang, you monster! You made me eat my cousin!" The other scholars were rousing as well, flinging similar accusations.

To Weijing's surprise, Guchang didn't respond immediately, just stared blankly at the scholars. Bull and his bandits reacted slowly as well, weaving and shuddering as if dizzied. Only Bull managed to stand, shouting, "Shut them up, Guchang! Shut them up now!"

"My, my, you are a strong one, aren't you? That *ranghe* syrup would incapacitate most *gu* demons," Officer Mei said as the servants who'd been assisting him tossed off their hooded robes to reveal uniforms of the Emperor's court. Weijing stared, because their faces remained the same. Had they been soldiers all along, then? Or was this part of Mei's sorcery?

As the soldiers went to take the bandits captive, Bull stumbled and crashed against the table. Dropping to his knees, he looked as if he were about to faint. Except Weijing knew him too well. "Look out!" he shouted as the bandit's darts cut the air, narrowly missing Mei.

Furiously, Bull swung his staff, intending to bash Weijing's skull in again. Only Officer Mei was there before the iron bar touched Weijing, a plain wooden staff blocking the weapon with a clang of metal on metal. "I don't think so, demon. I have use for the boy's brains still."

Weijing would have fled for the trees, once more in his flying squirrel form, but he owed a debt now. Bull was too big and strong an opponent for one as short and slight as Officer Mei. Grabbing the rug he'd been sitting on, he leapt over the table and flung one end in Bull's face.

As Bull roared furiously, rushing at Weijing, Mei poked him in the rear with his staff. When Bull swung around, Weijing swatted him in the back of the head. Back and forth they went, dodging and twisting, leaping and rolling, while Officer Mei's men laughed, sounding more like a pack of wild animals than humans.

At last, as Bull stumbled to a confused halt, Mei landed a good, solid, blow to the bandit's jaw. Knocked down, the man struggled, tried to sit up, tried again, then finally collapsed in a snoring heap.

"That was exciting," Mei commented wryly. "And more than a bit of a waste of time." He looked at Weijing. "Well done, child. It's always good to keep one's head, even after it's removed from your shoulders."

Reflecting that the advice was easier given then taken, especially considering how much being beheaded hurt, Weijing shrugged. "You didn't have a chance without me."

Officer Mei chuckled. "Possibly true, though I promise you, I've fought bigger and uglier oxen than that one." He turned to find the oldest of Guchang's confused disciples. "You understand you've been tricked?"

"Where is he? I swear, I'll make him pay for what he's done." The man was too thin and fragile to swat a mosquito, much less deal with an evil sorcerer whose illusions had tricked him into eating his fellow scholars.

"He's fled." Mei gestured upwards, towards the cloud covered peak of the mountain. "And you and yours can't go there."

"But he...."

"I know. He used you. He murdered your friends and he tainted you with his sins. You were fooled and hurt and now you're sickened." As tears formed in the scholar's eyes, the officer put a hand on his shoulder. "You should go back to Huangshan City when morning comes. Tell Judge Li what you know. Tell him I order him, in the name of the Jade Emperor of Heaven, to send his men to clean up this mess he permitted to grow within sight of his domain."

"But what will you be doing? Why can't you go with us?" That was one of the others, a youngster who barely looked old enough to be on her own, much less seeking any sort of enlightenment.

"I will be going to Huanjing to hunt down Guchang, among other things." Mei gestured upwards and the scholars gasped. Weijing didn't bother looking. He knew what they saw; a city, its ramparts shining in rainbow colors in moonlight, tiny lights flickering as its inhabitants went about their business.

All floating in the sky high above the peak.

"What did you do back there?" Weijing wasn't quite as curious about the last few hours as he pretended. But he didn't want to think about their destination and he knew he couldn't argue Officer Mei out of the trip. Easier to focus his thoughts on other mysteries. "Did you kill the chef? At least you didn't feed her to us."

"I leave the feeding of lovers to their lovers to other, less scrupulous sorts," Mei answered. "She's tied up in the kitchen. I expect she's either given up or gnawed her hoof off to escape by now."

Refusing to contemplate the possibilities of anyone, including her husband, regarding the old nag as a lover, Weijing tried to stay on subject. "Then what was that banquet? And what did you mean by *ranghe* syrup?"

"The banquet was an old friend of mine's contribution. You'd like him. He eats shrine food, too. As for *ranghe*, that's a type of wild ginger efficacious against the Hermit's *gu* magic."

Gu magic was the blackest of sorceries and Weijing was suddenly afraid. "Is that what I learned from him?"

"No. Lucky for you, what you learned is pure transformative magic. *Gu* magic needs blood and pain to operate properly. That geas of yours is typical. An imp used to bind a victim to its creator's will. It would have eaten your heart out sooner or later."

The memory of the geas and what it'd done to him before made Weijing shudder. He did not, however, tell Officer Mei the truth, that the thing had eaten his heart on a regular basis. He didn't want to explain how, or why, he was still standing afterwards.

"And the soldiers? Where did they come from?" They couldn't be Guchang's servants. Those were surely too weak to be of use.

"They were old friends of mine who Guchang bound to his service. I fixed that, the same way I fixed your problem." When Weijing eyed Mei disbelievingly, the officer added, "They're stronger than they look, child. It was Guchang's curse kept them weak."

Looking at the soldiers, Weijing realized the man was right. Freed, they had a strange, wiry, grace to them. Some loped along behind Weijing and Officer Mei, while others clambered the rocks beside the trail as if born to them. And others, he was shocked to realize, leapt from one small tree to the next, laughing like children on an outing. One, with a huge nose, was poking his companion, a rangy red-head whose arms seemed almost a foot too long for his body. Yet another had a bushy beard and small, beady, eyes.

"Are they really soldiers from the Imperial Court?" Weijing found it hard to believe any commander would put up with this unruly lot. "Or is their armor another illusion?"

"They are now, and more than willing to help me out after what Guchang did to them." Officer Mei watched one man somersault over another with the indulgent air of a proud father.

"So you came here to deal with Guchang? To punish him for what he was doing and save your friends?"

"Let's just say his punishment is part of my duty." The answer was evasive and they both recognized it. "I need to go to Huanjing for other, more personal reasons. I made a mistake, a long time ago and I have to make up for it, no matter what the price."

Mei's voice held little emotion but when Weijing looked over at him, he saw a brief flash of sorrow so deep he didn't know what he could say to ease it. "Huanjing isn't a magical kingdom with the power to right all wrongs."

"Thank you, boy. I do know that much." The officer's sudden grin hid his pain entirely. "You may not believe me, but I've been there before. A very long time ago; it was an interesting and edifying experience."

"I'm sure you have. Everyone sees a bit of it in their dreams. But that doesn't make it a place to visit. Or stay."

By this time they were just about to the peak of the mountain, where a set of misty stairs rose into the clouds. Weijing stared at them, finding it hard to believe they were actually there. Admittedly, he'd never tried to go back to Huanjing after he'd leapt from its misty heights. Nor, for that matter, did he want to now. If it weren't for Mei's insistent presence he'd have turned and run back down the mountainside. Maybe if he transformed?

Before the thought fully formed in Weijing's head, the officer's fingers closed on his earlobe. "No, baby boy. Papa needs you to be brave."

Once again Weijing yearned to snap that he wasn't Officer Mei's child and once more he didn't dare. "I'm not at all brave and I want to go back to Huangshan City."

"Sometimes you have to face the thing you fear most to get what you need, boy." There was an odd note in the man's voice, as if he were speaking to himself as much as to Weijing.

"I'd rather not need anything that badly, Officer Mei."

"Lucky for you, then, that you don't." The man sighed and called out to his soldiers. "This is where we part, old friends. Long Nose, keep an eye on them for me."

"You'll be all right in there? You won't need us?"

"Long Nose, you can't go where I'm going. Wait. I'll keep my promise, though it breaks my heart to do so." Officer Mei embraced each of his friends, then caught hold of Weijing's hand. "Quickly, now, child. If we don't get into the city now we won't get in at all."

As Weijing reflected that he'd be perfectly fine with such an outcome, Mei dragged him up the cloudy stairs, the thirty or so soldiers calling out as they ran. "Brother, beloved brother! Victorious in Strife! Remember us. Remember!"

Their voices faded away as the mists closed in.

Huanjing's streets were a confused maze of paths, combining aspects of dozens of different places. A mountain trail here, a flat lakeside walkway there. Even roadways that bent at impossible angles, where strange birdlike people walked sideways.

The walls of Huanjing glittered in the bright sunlight, glowed in the soft moonlight and glowered in utter darkness. Mirrors flickered into being as they passed, reflecting images Weijing knew weren't real. A robed man rode a strange dragon-like beast, companioned by a pig and a demon. A white-haired man twisted in smoke, screaming in pain as he burned from within. Two men battled soldiers armed with strange weapons, their fate fixed despite their strangely forged brotherhood. A one-armed fighter cut down rank upon rank of bandits, forcing his way across a wooden bridge. A girl carrying a sword hilt ran, leaving her brother to be rent asunder by a black garbed demon. An old man rode the back of a huge youngster, racing down a road as fast as his legs could carry him.

"You'll never find what you need there," Weijing told Officer Mei, noticing him stop to admire a pair of fighters breaking the arms of a white-garbed warrior. "Or in any of these. They're just illusions. Everything here is."

Mei tapped a mirror. "Awfully solid... Yah....." The mirror's surface rippled, dragging him forward. Only Weijing's quick grab drew him back before he was pulled in. "That might have been exciting. Though I'm almost sure I'd rather not wind up like those poor souls in there." The image in the mirror showed a half-dozen young women, their throats torn out by *jiangshi*, bleeding out into a huge cauldron.

"You don't. You'd survive. You always survive. But you're stuck until the dreamer wakes." Weijing picked his way down the street, searching for the safest path. He was about to beckon for Mei to follow when something flung itself through the air. A tangled mass of purple and black, it slammed into the officer and threw him headfirst into yet another mirror. Before Weijing could react, the glass shattered into several dozen pieces, the shards flying into other mirrors.

A figure rose up from the mist, surrounded by small bug like creatures with spikey 'hair' and greasy purple hides. "Well now, traitor boy. I believe it's just the two of us," Guchang announced with an air of grim satisfaction.

Without hesitation, because he knew what Guchang would do to him, Weijing leapt into the nearest mirror.

The dream landed Weijing on a rocky path overlooking an expanse of lava. "Wukong," a voice said wearily. "Please don't tell me you've found more trouble. We don't have time for your nonsense. We need fish paste to build a bridge across the lava."

Weijing raised his eyes to stare at the speaker; a bald man on the dragon horse. A the pig-faced man and demon stood beside him. "Cross? The lava?" He straightened and was unsurprised to find himself dressed in a suit of yellow fabric, a long tail flicking behind him. A piece of glass glittered at his feet and almost absentmindedly he picked it up and stuck it in his pouch.

"Yes. Cross. The lava. We must continue west if we are to fetch the scriptures."

"Wouldn't a fan be better than fish...." Weijing stopped himself. It was so easy to take the dreamer's role and be trapped. "No. Not this time! Not again!" Weijing leapt past the trio, over a rock and into a forest. The trees were covered in bright leaves and it took him a moment to realize the things were actually butterflies. Somewhere behind him, a voice yelled, "Come back, Monkey! Come back!"

Experience had taught Weijing better. He neither answered nor returned. He could feel the dream shifting around him, thickening the air and making it hard to move. It'd end soon enough, he knew. Dreamers didn't keep to a thought for very long. He just needed to separate dream logic from his own to stay free. Besides, the one thing he didn't want was to get tangled up in the Monkey King's strange tale. He didn't belong there and he knew it.

Keeping dream logic from taking over was easier said than done. Sleeping minds could rouse when a dream became too intense or dangerous. Those caught in the mists awake, however, could only wait for the dream to end. Worse, Weijing could hear a familiar scrabbling in the underbrush. Guchang's pets, searching around for him. The hermit's tools knew his scent, had found him before, when he'd tried to run away the first time.

The fact that Guchang could operate here, in the tangled confusion that was someone's dream, told Weijing something he would have preferred not be true. The hermit knew this landscape as well as Weijing did. He knew how to navigate its tricks and evade its traps. If Weijing was to escape, he'd have to outwit Guchang and his tools.

A house rose up in front of Weijing. He would have gone around, but he realized Guchang's pets were too close. Turn from his path now and he'd give them time to catch up. Inside, well, he'd be at the mercy of the dreamer's thoughts but safe from Guchang for a little while.

The building was strange, like nothing he'd ever seen in Huangshan City. The rooms were close and tight, decorated with odd twisted devices. A doorway blocked his path, a set of stairs ended in blank space. Another set of stairs went down, then up again, with no rhyme or reason to its path. An old woman watched him run past, saying something in a language he didn't understand.

The house went on for what seemed forever. It grew deeper and more twisted the further he went and he was just wondering if the dreamer would ever waken when he landed, flat on his face, on the misty pavement of Huanjing. He rolled on his back, ignoring the crackle of glass from the shattered piece of mirror he carried.

Guchang's pets roused Weijing a moment later and he forced himself to his feet. He needed a safe and quiet spot to think and Guchang wasn't going to give him that. He scanned his surroundings and made up his mind. Mist-walking here was probably the riskiest thing he'd ever tried, given the stiff breeze that constantly whipped down the streets, but it was the only way he was going to escape.

He flung himself upwards and let the wind take him where it willed.

Where the wind willed turned out to be the top of a tall tower at the bottom of the city. In the real world, of course, such a thing was physically impossible but this was Huanjing and nothing made sense. He sat against solid air, ignoring the big black crow cawing incessantly at him. They didn't like him much, those crows, though he'd never done anything to hurt them.

The first step was to decide what to do about Officer Mei. A part of Weijing was tempted to leave the man where he was. Trapped in someone else's dream, or someone else's story, Mei couldn't do anything to interfere with Weijing's life anymore. It wasn't as if he owed the man anything. Well, except for removing Guchang's geas, that was, and that account could be considered paid already.

Yet some small part of him, the lonely part that had never had a parent's guidance or a friend's companionship, didn't want to abandon the officer. He'd formed a sneaking liking for Officer Mei, quirky sense of humor and all. Besides, if he helped the man, Mei might, in turn, help rid him of Guchang.

Taking the shard from his pouch, Weijing tried to spot the officer inside it. No luck. He'd need the whole mirror to find Mei. Which, in turn, meant he'd have to explore the dozens of dreams the shards had fallen into.

Fortunately, he didn't have to go back to where he'd been to do so. Like everything else in Huanjing, the mirrors shifted position randomly. He'd been lucky to enter the right mirror first time, earlier. And now that he had a shard, he could use it to find the others. He just had to avoid Guchang while he hunted.

✝✝✝

The next mirror containing part of Officer Mei's self hung in a hall of gold and silver. An orchard lay beyond, where a beautiful Goddess tended almost the same peach trees Weijing had once gorged himself on, before self-awareness had come to him and he'd realized how empty his world really was.

"Sun Wukong! How dare you steal my fish! How dare you be a kaiju in my garden!"

Weijing had no idea how fish could grow in place of peaches, nor what a kaiju was. He couldn't even tell why a dozen tiny boxes were throwing stones at him. Nor did he care. He snatched up the next mirror shard and ran off again to wait for the dream to end so he could move on.

Again and again he repeated the task. Again and again he found himself caught in the role of the Monkey King. The dreams were never quite right, of course, but they all bore passing resemblances to the stories the street-performers told of the Stone Monkey. Weijing hadn't listened well to those tales, but he recognized the framework nonetheless. Monkey's birth from a stone. Monkey's claiming Fruit and Flower Mountain as his own. Monkey trapped beneath the palm of Buddha until he was ready to repent. All intertwined with an odd theme of fish. He couldn't guess why, but he supposed it didn't matter.

Every time Weijing found a shard, Guchang's pets found him and he barely managed to escape. Until, at last, he found himself in a royal bedchamber, a woman he felt he should know in his arms. After so many dreams reflecting the tales of the Monkey King, this one was entirely new. Only when the woman called him by name, Sun Wukong, did he realize he was still caught in the rôle.

This time it was terrifyingly difficult to break free of the dream. Weijing didn't want the woman as a lover. Some instinct in him said he shouldn't. But the Wukong whose rôle he'd fallen into desired her as he'd desired nothing else in all his life. Nothing could defeat that need. Neither fist nor thought could break him out of the dream.

The woman cradled Weijing's head against her and he was trapped by another desire altogether. A vague memory, lost in the confusion Huanjing created, made him press close, yearning for nothing more than to be cradled, safe and warm, in her protective arms.

Entranced, Weijing couldn't defend himself from the grasping claws of Guchang's pets. They found him. They gathered close. And in the end, they buried their fangs in his flesh and dragged him away, weeping for his mother.

Away and back to Guchang once more.

Guchang's pets dragged Weijing into a darkened cave, the only light coming from torches that glowed a sickly purple black. Some might think they'd been pulled back into the real world but Weijing knew better. Huanjing looked beautiful, a city of illusive confusion, but like any dream, it had a darker, uglier, side.

The cavern was one Weijing recognized, for it had connections to every aspect of Huanjing. There were hundreds of doorways, leading to the bright and shining ramparts of Heaven, where Gods and Immortals walked, to the deepest and darkest depths of the myriad hells. He could see the names on the doors and knew the one he wanted most. Reality, a plain wooden door with nothing to recommend it but life itself.

A voice spoke then, drawing Weijing's attention sideways to where a figure stood upside down beside him. "Little traitor, did you think you could truly escape me? I've watched your course and guided it for longer than you know."

Blearily, Weijing stared at the hermit, realizing it was he who was upside down, a cookpot bubbling beneath him. Again. Terror set him twisting and struggling. Trying not to breathe the fumes rising from its roiling black contents. A skull bobbed up, empty eyes staring helplessly. A hand stretched out, begging for help. It fell back in, though, revealing its owner had melted away in the sludge. A hazel eye rose next and Weijing shrieked, recognizing it.

With a laugh, Guchang held up a shard of mirror. "You've served me well despite yourself, traitor, gathering his pieces for me." He tossed the shining glass into the pot and a snaky object floated up. It took Weijing a moment to recognize a furry tail.

The thick fumes rising from the pot made mist-walking impossible. As for transformations, Weijing tried but found he was too tangled in Guchang's pets to break free. "No." he whispered. "Let me go." What little courage he possessed melted away, leaving him a terrified child expecting to be gutted and eaten. Again. Why, oh why, had he eaten those damned peaches anyway? Immortality without invulnerability was a curse, not a blessing.

"Not while I still have use for you, child born of dream." Guchang grinned at Weijing's expression. "Oh, yes, I always knew what you were. Where you came from. Who you were. I helped create you, after all, to hold my prey in the arms of your mother. He thought he slew me, but desire can never die."

"Mother? I don't have a mother."

"She was as much a dream as you, boy. You were the bait to my trap and now I have my fish in my pot. He thought he could escape. Desire will eat him up and leave nothing but the bones."

From the looks of it, Guchang had already gotten a head start on the job. The bits and pieces of Officer Mei were mere fragments. Even the bones were melting into sludge, a particularly foul soup-base. That wasn't the worst of it. Mei ought to be dead by now. Even in dream a human's mind couldn't take such treatment and survive. Yet the eye that kept popping up out of the stew insisted on looking at Weijing pleadingly, as if its owner could still see and beg for help.

...and now I have my fish in my pot.

Remembering what Mei had said about keeping one's head even when one lost it, Weijing realized he'd been wrong to think the man knew nothing of mortal wounds that didn't kill. His own experience gave him hope. It'd take some doing, getting the officer out of the pot, but once he was, whatever kept Mei alive would—hopefully—do its work. Of course, first all his parts had to be thrown in.

Swinging around, pretending to struggle, Weijing watched Guchang drop mirror shard after mirror shard into the mix. If he could get one hand free, he could reach the pot and spill its contents to the ground. Trying to distract Guchang, he gasped, "You can't have had me under control every minute."

"You think because you got away from my mountain I couldn't watch you? Foolish child. I saw everything you've done. Including that item you squirreled away. Speaking of which...." Guchang reached up and pulled Mei's scroll from Weijing's shirt. "I even saw you pretending to read this nonsense. As if you understood a word of it."

Guchang's mockery told Weijing more than the hermit meant to. He may have watched Weijing when he was down off the mountain and after his return, but Guchang didn't know everything. Weijing's only real teacher had been the scholar who'd taught him to read. He even knew how to write, though not well. The poor man had been handed over to Guchang's chef before he'd managed to show Weijing more than the basic strokes.

The memory of the scholar, and his kindness to a ill-favored serving boy did what nothing else Weijing had experienced could do. He'd tried to forget the rage, but watching Guchang gloat, seeing the man so sure he'd gotten away with his foul plot, brought it all back. When Guchang tossed the scroll into the fire and a faint groan of protest bubbled out of the liquid, Weijing knew what he had to do.

It wouldn't kill him. Nothing ever did. But it was going to hurt like nothing had hurt before. Still, driven by rage and need, Weijing transformed to mist and dropped into the pot with Officer Mei. As the heat seared him and the liquid intertwined with his Self, he transformed again. This time to an ogre.

The pot was big, but not big enough to take the strain. It exploded, pieces of metal shrapnel flying through the room.

Someone had slung Weijing over their shoulder. Officer Mei, wearing nothing but a robe wrapped tight round his waist, a few bones and muscles sticking out where they'd yet to regenerate. Oh, yes, and a bedraggled tail hanging behind him like a well-used washcloth.

Weijing stared at the thing blankly. He wasn't thinking clearly, still coughing and wheezing from taking a bit too much of Officer Mei soup into his lungs. "Tail? You have a tail?"

"So it seems. You really do need to work on that mist-walk, boy."

Weijing ignored the man's gentle scold in favor of complaining, "Reality was that way."

"No doubt. But there are two reasons I'm not going there. First, I didn't come to Huanjing to go back without finishing my job."

"You mean stopping Guchang wasn't your job?"

"He's one of my jobs and always will be. But I've another, far more important one. Though I'm not sure how I'm going to manage it, now."

Officer Mei's voice had a worried note and Weijing guessed it was the scroll's destruction that troubled him. Not daring to ask, he returned to the earlier topic. "You said two reasons."

"Have you bothered to look behind us? Instead of at my poor tail?"

Startled, Weijing looked up to see thousands of purple imps racing after them, casting long black shadows in the cavern's dim light. Guchang was further back, looking as if he'd been dropped in a slime pit. Or, Weijing corrected himself, as if a slime pit had dropped onto him. Which wasn't far from the truth. "Can you go faster?"

"And risk losing him? I may as well kill two birds with one stone here. If he's fool enough to follow me where we're going, let him."

Weijing peered at the doors as they passed, struggling to read their names in the dim light. Hell of the Adulterers. Hell of the Usurers. Hell of Torturers. "ARE YOU OUT OF YOUR MIND?"

"Oh, quite likely. Had my brains squeezed a few times too many a while back and now I think I have to save everyone." Mei laughed. "Don't worry. We're almost there." He skidded to a halt and set Weijing down. "You'll have to open the door for me, though. I'm not allowed."

Weijing stared at the door, a grand, red-lacquer affair that didn't need a single word for him to know where it led. "You really are mad."

"I did just admit to it. Will you please open the door, child? Papa has work to do."

Yet again, Weijing ignored Mei's jibe. He didn't see any reason why the man wanted to go to hell so badly but given that they were being chased and with the hope they'd lose Guchang here, he opened the door and stepped through. Into the Court of the Yama King.

✝✝✝

The grand hall beyond the door was oddly familiar and Weijing realized it reflected Huangshan City's court. It was bigger and more elaborate, but with soldiers standing to the side at attention and the red-faced man sitting at the table at the far end, its resemblance was a little too close to reality.

Things skittered through the door after Weijing and Mei; purple imps that exploded as soon as they entered. Weijing jerked with each loud pop but Officer Mei, insouciant as ever, ambled forward.

"You again! You are not welcome in this place." The Yama King, and it had to be he, glared down furiously. "Not after all the trouble you caused us last time. Tearing out a whole page, just because you felt like it."

"I thought you used an inkbrush," Weijing muttered, realizing who Mei had to be.

"Same story, different props." Mei waved off the question. "Now, now, Your Majesty. I even stood in for you back in the day."

"That wasn't you. That was your dream, you aggravation."

"Dreams have power, or Huanjing wouldn't exist, now would it? Nor the path I took to get here." A few larger explosions behind them forced Mei to pause until Guchang's pets had finished popping out of existence. "Sorry about the mess. Would you like me to clean it up?"

"Never mind that. What are you doing here?"

Weijing turned to watch Guchang rush through the door after them, having failed to recognize where he was. The hermit skidded to a halt, then screeched, "King Yama! That man has interfered with the course of fate!" From his expression, he was trying his best to regain control of the situation.

King Yama eyed Guchang as he came forward. Then he beckoned for a large book and flipped through it. "Let's see. You're... ah, here you are. Qing the Fish. A demon of desire."

The hermit's mouth worked. "I? You? What? I can't be in there! I'm immortal!"

"Of course you can be," Officer Mei countered. "Even desire can fade and die."

The whole situation felt like yet another dream. Weijing wondered if he was still searching for pieces of Officer Mei in Huanjing's mirrors. "What are we here for?"

"You and I are here to pass through that door there." Mei indicated a gate on which the words, "Human World" were written. "Leaving desire behind us, of course." Seeing Weijing's confusion, the man added, "A long time ago, this demon here tried to trap me in a dream, a marvelous dream, where I fell in love and fathered many children. It was grand fun and I was sorry it had to end, but I had a responsibility and a life to protect."

Guchang sneered. "You gave up power and love and fatherhood, all to drag some fool monk across the mountains and back for a bunch of meaningless scribbles."

"They weren't meaningless to those who wanted them. And I only regret the latter two. Lust for power was never my downfall." Mei shrugged off the complaint. "Your Majesty, you know how much trouble I can be. Wouldn't it be best for all if you let me and the boy here pass?"

"Not so fast, nuisance. You committed sacrilege the last time you were here. You don't think I'm going to let you through unless you restore that stolen page to its place."

Weijing swallowed. "Was it written on bamboo slats?"

"Of course. What else would they be written on?" The Yama King slammed the book open and swung it around to show the 'pages', thin slips of bamboo sewn together with red silk. Just like the scroll Guchang had destroyed.

The hermit laughed mockingly. "Of course. So it was important, was it? Valuable to you... 'Officer Mei'? How do you plan on getting past this one, you stupid fool?"

"A good question." Mei spread his hands, trying to look unconcerned. But Weijing caught a glimpse of pain in his bright gold eyes. The same look had crossed Mei's face before, speaking of mistakes he'd made. "Your Majesty? What would you have me do?"

"You could write them down again," the Yama King suggested and there was almost a note of sympathy in his voice.

"Can't. I haven't looked at those pages for a long time now. Even if there were a place to put the names, I wouldn't remember them all."

"I could." Weijing's interjection made everyone stare at him and he tried not to cower behind Officer Mei.

"You're an illiterate peasant, boy," Guchang snapped.

"Scholar Tian Ci taught me before you cooked him for dinner." Weijing turned to Mei and saw a brief flash of hope in the man's eyes. "He taught me to memorize what I read, too. I read the scroll, I remember the names."

The Yama King examined Weijing's earnest expression and drew out a fresh sheet of bamboo slats. "Write them, then. If you can fill this properly, I will permit you and this nuisance to go as he asks."

Someone brought ink and a table and Weijing knelt, closing his eyes to remember each detail. "Long nose", he wrote. "Bushy beard." Name after name, carefully, if inexpertly written. Until there was space for but one more.

"You must fill the page, boy. Otherwise the bargain's off and you two stay here."

Weijing shook his head. "That was the last name, though. I've put every name on that page down."

"Even so."

Humorously, Officer Mei said, "What about mine?"

Weijing blinked. Tried to remember the officer's chop from his release form. He was about to write it down when he realized just how bad an idea it would be. Meiyou Ren meant nobody and if nobody died, the world would get very full, very quickly. Cautiously, he asked, "Could one of you fine gentlemen tell me how to write the word for surname?"

For a moment he thought Officer Mei would choke, he looked so worried. But, even so, he took the brush and wrote the word for Weijing to copy. "Do you need the rest?" he asked, in a resigned sort of way, while Guchang laughed up his sleeve.

Weijing took the brush back. "No. You gave me those back at Huangshan City." Then, before he could lose his nerve, he wrote "Sun Weijing" in the last blank space.

The Yama King eyed Weijing thoughtfully as he brought the scroll forward and placed it in the God's hands. "Are you sure?"

"I've eaten too many peaches to die easily," Weijing said. "I know that. But I don't want to never die. And I don't think my name is in your book yet, is it?"

"Sadly, no. A child born in dream can't die because he was never truly born." Taking the page, the Yama King placed it in his book, where it sealed itself into place.

Instantly, the room was full of soldiers, or, rather, monkeys dressed as soldiers. "You did it, brother! We're back. We can be part of the cycle again!" the one called Long Nose called, catching Officer Mei by the shoulders. Trapped by several monkeys and apes, Guchang swore and struggled.

"Should we eat him?" Long Arms asked, baring huge fangs and clutching Guchang tight.

"No. He can't follow us."

"The hell I can't!"

Before Guchang could struggle free, the Yama King waved a hand. "I think not, Qing fish. You haven't earned your release just yet." His soldiers caught hold of the hermit and dragged him off, screaming angrily.

Quickly, Mei embraced each of his old friends then caught hold of Weijing's hand. "Come with papa, boy. Just because you can die doesn't mean you have to just yet. And there's so much world out there to show you."

Before anyone could stop them, given they even tried, Mei dragged Weijing through the gate and back into the human world.

†††

Once again, Weijing found himself falling. Only this time a pair of arms caught him and carried him to Huangshan peak, the morning sun just turning the sky a lovely shade of tangerine. "Now if that doesn't make one hungry, nothing will," Mei said, searching around for the path down. "You know, I'd have given you my name if you'd asked for it."

"I know. But you earned your immortality. You don't belong on that page anymore." Weijing followed the man down the trail. "And all I did was be born in a dream."

"And eat far more peaches than is good for any one person."

"And eat far more peaches than is good for any one person."

They continued down, Officer Mei turning to a gold-furred monkey and leaping from tree to tree. Challenged, Weijing took his favorite form, gliding past the officer on red-furred skin-flaps.

"I still don't know why you won't be a monkey. You're my son, you know. Or you were in that dream Guchang gave me, all those years ago."

It was true, but Weijing had gotten used to the squirrel shape and he rather enjoyed soaring through the air this way. "Find me a monkey with wings and I'll think about it." He paused, adding, worriedly, "I was right, then, thinking you're the Monkey King?"

"Sun Wukong. Great Sage, Equal to Heaven," Officer Mei agreed cheerfully. "Bodhisattva, Victorious in Strife. And...."

"And?"

"And more importantly, your father. Of a sort. Which, Gods help us all, makes me responsible for you. Until you grow up, at least."

They leapt into the forest, a monkey and a squirrel, looking for adventure and knowing they wouldn't have to go far to find it.

THE END

Just Monkeying Around

I've always had a soft touch for the Trickster. He (it's usually, but isn't always, a he) is the goofball troublemaker who changes the world, pushes the boundaries and, quite often, falls over his own two (or more) feet when his trick blows up in his face.

So when Ron announced he was looking for stories for his new Mythology Anthology, I knew I wanted in. And, given I've been drawing on my love of Chinese tales in my other works, I figured this might be a great time to try out a Monkey King tale.

The Monkey King, AKA, Sun Wu Kong, AKA, The Great Sage Equal to Heaven, is one of those characters from Chinese Myth who had managed to make a name for himself all over the world. Although he's primarily a Buddhist figure, he has ties to Daoism as well. Of course, the story we know best comes from Wu Cheng'en's novel "Journey to the West", the tale of his transformation from a troublemaking monkey seeking immortality to a Bodhisattva.

Once I'd settled on making the Great Sage the protagonist of my story, I had to decide where in his tale I needed to write. Which, of course, meant I had to research "Journey to the West" and other works. As I've noted elsewhere, Research is Fun and this was no exception to the rule. I re-read a decent translation of the book and in the course of my investigations, learned there were sequels. One, "A Supplement to Journey to the West", by Dong Yue, was particularly interesting.

In the work, Monkey runs into a Dream Demon and is nearly trapped in a fantastic and surreal reality. There he is dragged through dream after dream where he becomes enamored of Princess Iron Fan, gets to play substitute Judge of Hell, and become a general leading an army against his own sons. In the end, he realizes he's dreaming and manages to escape.

Out of such little tidbits are stories made and this was no exception. I'd long had a character in my head who was the Monkey King's son and this gave me the excuse I needed to use him. "Tales from a Chinese Studio" by Pu Songling gave me a location and my love of Wuxia movies gave me the visuals.

With all those factors thrown together I couldn't help but have a blast with this. I do hope it's as much fun to read as it was to write.

BARBARA DORAN—has been making up stories for as long as she can remember. From playing Ms. Marvel to her best friend's Captain Marvel to writing new stories for old characters (Hannibal King, X-Men, Green Hornet, The Saint, The Shadow and many others), to writing gaming and anime fanfiction online.

After ten years behind the keyboard as a software engineer, Barbara realized that her true love wasn't coding but making stuff up. So when she left that career in favor of dealing with two frequent interruptions of her life (namely her own personal Tiger and Dragon), she decided to use what little time they allowed her to work on writing. Her Long Suffering Husband, without whom she could never have managed such a goal, has been nothing if not supportive.

Along with reading every mystery, SF and fantasy book she could get her hands on, Barbara grew up watching Star Trek, Batman, Green Hornet, along with the usual Saturday morning cartoons. She became addicted to shows like Battle of the Planets and Doctor Who in her teens and discovered Run Run Shaw's martial arts flicks some years later. Those influences, along with a love of folklore and mythology, have become part of the world some small portion of her mind lives in. When, of course, she isn't chasing Tiger and Dragon from one school event to another.

Barbara can be contacted at <BarbaraDoran@sumergoscriptum.com>. Her website is <http://www.sumergoscriptum.com/barbaradoran/>.

Beowulf: The Schemes of Unferth

BY
FRED ADAMS, JR.

Unferth slogged through the fetid brown water of the bog at the heart of Deep Forest, wary of every step lest he slip and fall into the slimy muck that sucked at his feet. The Witch's Fen was no place to wear mail and plate. Should he fall, he could easily drown before he could escape the weight that pressed him into the muddy bottom. He had hidden his armor under the tree roots that hung in the air from an eroded bank like clutching talons and gone forth in leggings and a jerkin. Wisps of mist rode from the fen's surface and above him, thick clouds turned the sun into a cold white eye that stared uncaring whether he lived or died. The tepid swamp soaked him to the waist and his skin itched at the very thought of what disease rode the foul water through his clothing.

Defeat in combat, even death by the sword he could bear, but to be humiliated and brushed aside as irrelevant, to be made insignificant in front of his people was unforgivable. The arrogant bastard who insulted him would pay and pay dearly for the slight.

A touch at his leg; something slithered against him just slowly enough to let him know it was feeling him out, to learn whether he was predator or prey. He froze for a moment, clutching his sword with a white knuckled hand, his eyes frantically searching the surface for any trace of the unseen threat. A coil of meat and bone whipped around his leg under the water as the snake's flat ugly head broke the surface. A scaly horror, its visage was more human than reptile with a mouth full of fangs like shards of broken pottery.

The serpent struck at Unferth's throat, and he deflected the strike with the flat of his sword as he felt the body of the snake coiling around his other leg, trying to pull him off his feet. It feinted, striking at his face, and when Unferth raised his sword to block it, the head darted downward, sinking full-fanged into his thigh. Unferth screamed and swept downward with his blade, severing the head from the crushing coils. The body fell away thrashing, but the head lived on, its jaws working with the last of its life to pump its venom deeper into Unferth's body. Unferth battered the leathery skull with the pommel of his sword, spattering the murky water with brains and gore and finally breaking bone and knocking away the clamping jaws.

With trembling fingers, he pulled two of the creature's fangs from his thigh. The burning pain of the venom was spreading, and he knew the blood in the water would summon more of the snake's kind or other horrors. He had to move on and do so quickly. He sliced a strip of leather from his jerkin and tied it tightly between the wound and his hip to slow the flow of the venom with his blood toward his heart. Already his leg was numb but he pushed onward in the hope that he would reach the witch's cave before the leg gave out and he fell to never rise again.

Ahead of him, the water bubbled and roiled. He stared as a head emerged from the water. It was black; no, not just black, but seemed an absence of light and from its angular face, red eyes glowed from sloping lids. The figure stood, and Unferth thought at first it was a boy by its height then realized the wasted sinew and muscle that knotted the misshapen arms and torso belonged to a creature as old as the swamp. He raised his sword to defend himself against this new threat when it spoke with a voice like a cracked horn. "Put aside your sword, good Unferth. I am Gogalog. I mean you no harm. You seek Mistress Magda, do you not?"

Unferth could barely speak. "Yes. I seek Magda the Witch."

"Then I will take you to her." The black man seized Unferth's wrist and with a grip belying his look, pulled Unferth under the water and dragged him through a hole in the bottom of the fen. In an instant, Unferth stood in a stony grotto dimly lit by smoky pine splints. He gagged as he choked out the brackish water he had swallowed.

"Follow me, good Unferth, and you shall meet the one you seek." Unferth limped behind the dark minion over the rough stone floor and into a dark corridor. They followed twists and turns, passing black warrens and side passages from which hungry eyes glowed. Unferth gripped his sword tighter. Gogalog laughed, a thick, gurgling sound in the close passageway. "You have no need to fear the Mistresses' pets, good Unferth, so long as you please her."

Light glowed beyond a bend in the passageway. As the light became stronger, so did the stench of burning flesh and hair until Unferth could barely breathe. He and Gogalog turned the corner and stepped into a high-ceilinged room hewn from the rock. Foul water from the swamp overhead dripped from the ceiling and splashed coldly on his bare head. The source of the light and the stench were the same. Bodies of men and women were tied to stakes, their heads set afire like torches. Unferth thought they were dead until one of them let out a ghastly choking scream.

In the center of the room, on a crude chair upon a dais sat a bundle of sticks covered in rotting parchment and rags. Gogalog knelt before it. "Mistress." The bundle stood taking a roughly human form and Unferth swooned, almost fainting. "Welcome, good Unferth," it said, in a voice like rustling weeds. "Why do you seek poor old Magda?"

Summoning his courage, Unferth said, "I seek your help to destroy an enemy."

"And this enemy's name?"

"Beowulf."

"*That* one!" Magda spat and where her rancid gob struck, the floor bubbled like acid on iron. "That one killed my half-sister and her son and her minions. Yes, I will help you destroy him, but first, we must save you."

Magda stepped from the dais with a dry rustle of bones and rags. "The bite of a fen serpent brings palsy and delirium before a long and agonizing death. Show me your wound." Unferth unbound the leather strip and tore open his legging. In the dim light he could see the raw bite marks ringed with oozing purple welts. The witch touched a black scabrous tongue to her sprig of an index finger and rubbed it slowly three times around the infected rings chanting in a low whisper. Gradually, the swelling abated and the dark rings faded. As Unferth watched in wonder, the bite marks closed over and disappeared as if he had never been bitten.

Magda cocked a glittering eye at the thane. "If my skill surprises you, good Unferth, why did you come to me?"

"One can hear of a marvel yet still marvel at its sight."

The witch cackled. "You are a clever man, Unferth. Your words serve you where your war prowess fails. You keep your position and your head while others lose theirs. Tell me why you wish Beowulf to be destroyed."

"He has become too popular and too powerful for his murderous deeds. King Hrothgar took him as a son, and although that is an honorary title at best, Beowulf is adored by the people who yet see him as an infallible hero. It is feared that he may aspire to seize the throne for himself with little opposition."

"And why are you so suddenly patriotic, my worthy thane?" Magda's voice dripped with sarcasm. "I ken there is more."

"I am told you see all. If you already know, why do you ask?"

"To learn whether the petitioner pleads his case with prejudice or shows all faces of the truth. One lies by withholding as surely as he does by dissembling. Speak true to me or—" Magda gestured with her twig of an arm around the cave at her human torches.

"Hrothgar is not long for this life. Hrethric will be crowned—"

"Ahh, now we see one root of the poisonous bush. Go on."

"And Hrothulf, Horthgar's younger son would be king. But Beowulf has pledged his support to Hrethtric and sworn to train and aid him in his rule."

"This plot is a many-headed snake. Why should you care who rules? One foot upon your neck should feel little different from another."

"Because Hrothulf will make me his advisor and I will rule through him."

"And?"

"And I would have my revenge upon Beowulf for humiliating me before my kin and fellows. I was the pride of my people before he came. None held more glory and esteem. The bastard son of Egctheow mocked me before he did battle with Grendel. When I questioned his valor by recounting his contest with the stout hearted Breca, he said I was drunk and mead was the fount of my boldness. He accused me of murdering my kinsmen and said I was damned."

"All true," hissed Magda. "And truth is a swift arrow to the heart of pretense, is it not, good Unferth? Perhaps your fame was not so truly conveyed."

Unferth's face reddened.

Magda waved a frail hand and threw a pinch of powder into the flames of one of her torches. A thick green smoke billowed from the fire and coalesced into the figure of Beowulf himself. So real it seemed that Unferth raised his sword in defense. Beowulf stood full height, the torchlight dancing on his war-worn mail shirt and greaves. His thick arms were crossed, and beneath the brim of his helm, his blue eyes blazed from a snake's nest of scars.

Beowulf spoke. "Unferth," his voice boomed and echoed in the cavern, "I boast not when I say that neither you nor Breca were ever much celebrated for swordsmanship or in facing danger on the field of battle. You killed your own kith and kin, so for all your cleverness and quick tongue, you will suffer damnation in the depths of hell. Unferth, if you were truly as keen or courageous as you claim to be, Grendel would never have got away with such unchecked carnage, attacks on your king, havoc in Heorot, and horrors everywhere. But he knew he need never be in dread of your blade making a mizzle of his blood."

The sounds of the Geats and the Danes' laughter bounced from the walls of the chamber and joined by the mocking howls of the demon hordes in the darkness of the caves. Unferth clapped his hands to his ears to shut out the sound, but it continued to reverberate inside his head. He roared and raised his sword, charging at the leering Beowulf. Unferth swung a cleaving stroke, and the image dissolved into the greenish smoke once again and faded away.

Unferth's breath heaved. His heart pounded in his chest, and Magda said, "Good! Good, my worthy thane. You have shown me your true heart in all of its hatred, and I can spin that thread of hate into a web that will bring down your nemesis."

"You will kill him?"

"No, Unferth, to simply kill him would deify him in the minds and hearts of your people; it would make him an icon that Hrethric need only name to rally the people behind him. Just as you struck the image of the death-dealer in this cave, must you strike the image of the man in Heorot. It is not enough that he die; he must first be ground to dust to show his worshippers that their hero can fall."

"How can that be? I gave him Hrunting, the great battle sword when he braved the cave of the monsters and slew Grendel's mother, knowing its blade would not be proof against magic and hoping he would die and I would be rid of him, but he found that damned rune sword made by the elves and hewed his way to glory to spite me. He has the luck of the gods on his shoulder."

Magda cackled. "Wyrd often saves a man if courage be good. That is a lesson you would do well to learn."

Unferth flushed, indignant. "I had the courage to come to this accursed place."

"Indeed, and we shall see whether Fate will be your friend or enemy."

Unferth smiled, his eyes gleaming with excitement. "He made his name with his sword arm. That is how he must fall. Make his sword arm soft as that of any man. Take away his might and brawn that he might be bested in combat."

"I shall," Magda said. "But you must not deign to fight him."

Unferth's brow creased in puzzlement. "I do not understand."

"Your purpose is twofold. To achieve one end without the other would be a hollow victory at best. If you bring down the hero, people will never forgive you, and your place under Hrothulf will be uneasy at best. A man who would kill his own brother for advantage would think even less of disposing of one not his kin, as well you know. You must summon an outsider to do the deed, and the sin of it will leave when the goat is driven from the land."

"You are wise in the ways of men, Magda."

"I have dealt with them for more lifetimes than you can imagine."

"You have not told me when this will take place, nor of a price for your service."

"To see the slayer of my kin grovel in shame and humiliation is payment enough. Summon your champion; by the time he arrives, Beowulf will no longer be able to fight him." The leathery face twisted into what passed for a smile. "However, there is another bargain I'd strike if you have the courage."

"What would that be, Mistress Magda?"

"Generations ago I was granted everlasting life without everlasting beauty, a blessing and a bane in one gift. I can renew my youth and beauty for one lifetime if the right man makes love to me, and the rewards for my lover will be beyond imagining. The last man to try was not so blessed." She waved a hand at Gogalog, who hung his dark head. Magda drew back the rags that covered her breast, baring a wizened dug that sagged like a slack purse. "So, good Unferth, are you the right man? Do you dare to roll the dice? Take the chance and be my lover." She held out her ancient arms to him, and Unferth backed away, repulsed, his hands palm up before him like a frightened child.

Magda threw back her head and laughed. "No?" she said, "then begone!" A dark cloud like smoke swirled around Unferth and in an instant, he was standing on the bank of the fen, beside the tree where he had left his mail and helm.

The sun was lower in the sky and Unferth moved quickly to return to Heorot. Beowulf had slain many monsters, but Unferth dared not brave the evils that still stalked Deep Forest in the dark.

Wiglaf found Beowulf sitting as he often did, at the edge of a huge outcrop overlooking the wild river and twisted trees many fathoms below. "Wiglaf, your step betrays you," said Beowulf without turning to confirm the identity.

"A stealthy step behind you could put one in peril, my lord."

Beowulf laughed heartily, and the rings of his mail jingled like dull bells. "Lord. Of all people, you should know I find the title unseemly."

"The King himself has made you his son; that puts the crown upon you, my friend, like it or not."

"But it is a wooden crown at best."

"It is not the substance of the crown but of the man who wears it that matters. You have no design on the throne; why not enjoy the moment and the good it brings with it? You are well fed, well treated and well regarded here, and still you have the freedom to take your leave when you wish. You are not bound for life to this place and these people as a successor would be. For once, accept the moment's good fortune at its face."

"Well spoken, Wiglaf, but comfort is not meant for such as we. The edge of the sword is where we belong, like the edge of this cliff, always a step from conflict and peril. I would sooner win a kingdom for another than rule one."

"Well spoken yourself, my friend, but as is often true, each side of the coin shows its own truth."

Beowulf chuckled. "If ever I am a king, Wiglaf, you will be my ambassador. Your words are as sharp as my blade." Beowulf rose to his full height, a head taller than Wiglaf. The warrior's eyes darkened as he kicked a pebble over the edge and watched it fall into the tangled trees below. "Yet for all we are and all we do, we are little more than that stone; Wyrd turns the wheel, and those of us at its top fall from even the greatest height to be crushed beneath it."

"Well, my friend," said Wiglaf, "Let us hope that neither of us falls before we gnaw at a haunch of that boar Athelread speared this morning. It turns on the spit as we speak."

The pair turned away from the ledge and started back to the mead hall, but Wiglaf paused to look back at the precipice one more time. When it came, and it would someday come, it would be a long fall indeed for them both.

Heorot, the great mead hall Hrothgar had built to reward his warriors and testify to his greatness, stood atop a bluff that sloped downward from all six of its sides, the more easily defended for its location and the view of the surrounding territory. The hall was built of rough-hewn logs and stood twenty cubits at its tallest, with a great fire pit at its center and a two-leaved iron bound door its only entrance. Formidable as it was, however,

Heorot was not proof against the devil-thing Grendel, the savage creature that ravaged Hrothgar's kingdom and slew his men with hellish abandon.

It was this Grendel that Beowulf slew; by the mighty grip of his hand he tore the arm from the monster that slunk back to the fens to die of its mortal wound. And when the beast's mother ravaged Heorot yet again for vengeance sake, Beowulf met her in her cave and killed not only the Hell-hag, but her brood of monstrous children. By this Beowulf saved Hrothgar's kingdom and for this, Beowulf was adopted by the king as a son.

Now Hrothgar sat less often on his throne or his chair at the great table, for age had dimmed his sight and clouded his mind. Two winters had passed since Grendel's death, and the old king would soon join him. But tonight, Hrothgar sat at the table bright-eyed with his young queen Wealtheow and his sons beside him.

The mead flowed and the laughter became more raucous as the men ate and drank into the night. Great boasts were made, and songs were sung about great deeds and battles. So many nights in the shuddering past, Hrothgar's people had eaten in silence, mourning the loss of their kindred to the monster Grendel, and fearing that the sounds of merriment would bring the hater of laughter to their hearth again. It was good to see life lived to the full once more.

"Our friend Unferth seems loath to join in our merriment," Wiglaf said. The King's son sat apart in a dark corner of the mead hall, his eyes in his cup.

"He is foolish," Beowulf said, "to fear me as a usurper of Hrothgar's throne. I am a son to Hrothgar by choice. Hrothulf and Hrethric are his sons by blood. Blood is the stronger tie."

"True, my friend," said Wiglaf, "but if choice were the strongest horse, the crown would rest on your head when Hrothgar breathes his last. Among the three of you, you are the most likely to hold and defend the kingdom that Hrothgar has struggled for so many years to maintain. You are the warrior that they are not."

"And Unferth is the schemer, the manipulator, the fabricator that I am not. The world we know changes, Wiglaf. In my father's time, a king ruled by the edge of his sword, led his people into battle. Today, a king rules by the edge of the sword, but not his own. In the days of my father, when a king could not defend his crown man to man against a challenge, he was no longer king. Today, a king buys his swords to do his fighting for him."

"And Hrothgar," said Wiglaf, gesturing across the fire to the throne

The mead flowed and the laughter became more raucous...

where Hrothgar sat, his young queen Wealtheow holding his cup. "Hrothgar may be able to lift his sword, but he could not defend a kingdom with it, yet all serve him faithfully."

"They serve from love, because he gives them gold and food and the shelter of Heorot. But they also serve him from respect for the force that made him king, tradition. None of these men would willingly rule himself. That would require of them discipline and accountability. They need a king they did not appoint so that they need not blame themselves when the kingdom fails."

Beowulf looked across the hall to the bench where Unferth cradled his cup in both hands, gazing into it as if to read his fate in its dregs. The king's son raised his eyes to meet those of Beowulf, and Unferth's lips curled in a cruel smile then embraced the rim of his cup.

"I am a sword wielder, a war thane who has killed many, man and monster, in my time," Beowulf said. "Unferth is a twister of men, a weaver of devious webs. There is no accounting for the number who may someday die by his machinations. As the wheel turns, which of us is the greater peril to the other?"

Unferth laughed. "My Lord, you always have the comfort that when all else fails, you can swing your fist and crush the head of your foe."

"So long as arm and courage persist."

"To that we drink," Wiglaf said, and he curled his arm around his friend's, and they drained their cups, as all around them Hrothgar's people laughed and roared, all but one.

That night as he lay on his pallet in the hall, sword by his side, Beowulf woke to the sound of a musical voice calling his name. His eyes opened to see a woman in a gossamer gown whose folds undulated like the fingers of an anemone. She glowed blue-white, floating in the air above him. He tried to raise his hands to push away the succubus, but his arms would not answer.

The beautiful creature extended her hand and traced a delicate finger from the shoulder of his sword arm to the tips of his fingers. Where the finger touched him, it traced a cold line that sank into him, muscle and bone. Then the lovely face bent to kiss him. The kiss was burning ice on his lips. Then the phantom drifted away as if borne by a gentle breeze and faded from view.

Beowulf sat up and looked around him in the dim glow of the fire pit embers. Around the hall, He saw the shapes of sleeping men, heard their snores and heavy breathing. He was awake. The visitation was no dream.

He lay, eyes open, on his pallet until morning, cold sweat dripping from his brow. What curse had the witch-thing laid upon him?

✝✝✝

The next day, he found out.

As they often did, Beowulf and his men patrolled the forests and fens around Heorot, seeking out bands of reivers and packs of savage nomads who would steal Heorot's sheep, its cattle, or its women. Two hills beyond the cultivated fields, Ragnar dropped to the ground.

"What do you see, Ragnar?" Beowulf said.

"The print of toes, my lord. A print like a great cat, but not like a great cat."

"You speak in riddles," Athelstead said.

"Perhaps a bear," said Wiglaf.

Ragnar shook his head. "No, the toes spread from the pad like a fan. The toes in a bear's print lie beside each other, and a bear's track shows claw marks. These show claw marks as well, an aspect of both in one."

"A combination of bear and cat in one beast?" Wiglaf snorted, but others in the party murmured with fear."A demon," one of Hrothgar's men whispered.

Beowulf crouched over the print and studied it carefully. "Whatever made this is no demon. It has form, and it has weight; no phantom made this print." He turned to Ragnar. "Look closely around you. See whether you can find other tracks like this one. The rest of you hold back. If there are more of these prints, I want them undisturbed."

Ragnar dropped to toes and fingertips and crept across the rocky ground. In a moment he called out, "My Lord, I have found another."

Beowulf and Wiglaf knelt beside a patch of bare earth and saw another of the tracks. "It is the same foot. See the crooked third toe." Ragnar crawled forward toward the trees at the edge of the clearing. "There are others, but something is wrong about them." He pointed to a pair of tracks side by side, as if made by a man. "The beast walks upright, and has two right feet."

"How can that be?" said Wiglaf.

"Why do you say two right feet?" Beowulf asked.

"This is no living creature, my lord. These tracks are like stamps from an ironmonger's die. They are identical. They —"

A piercing scream came from the trees. An egg-sized stone bounced off Ragnar's helmet with enough force to knock him over sideways. In seconds, Beowulf and his men were being pelted from every direction.

"Circle!" Beowulf shouted, dragging Ragnar to his feet. "Shields!" The men gathered back to back and raised their shields to the rattling stones as a shrieking horde of half-naked savages, faces painted like red skulls, burst from the brush at all sides. They brandished crude weapons; wooden clubs studded with animal fangs, spears that were little more than sharpened branches, axes made of flat stones lashed to sticks, and fist-sized rocks laced into leather thongs, but no less deadly for their lack of artifice.

The skull men shrieked as if one shrill voice and closed quickly on Beowulf and his men.

The fighting was fierce from both sides. The first of the skull-men to charge at Beowulf crashed into his shield, trying to bowl him over. Beowulf drew his sword and tried to raise it over his head, and found he could lift it no higher than his waist. Another skull-man ran at him with a spear. Beowulf twisted aside to avoid the point and spun back to crash his shield into the attacker's head, splitting it open.

Their weapons were crude, but the red-faced savages made up for that fact with their zeal and their numbers. One of them swung a head-sized stone in a net and swept the feet from two of Hrothgar's warriors, who crashed to the ground and were immediately beset by a pack of their enemies.

The thanes of Heorot hacked, slashed, and stabbed, and the savages fell by twos and threes, but their numbers gave them the advantage.

A studded club crashed into Wiglaf's shield, and the teeth in its head stuck in the banded wood. As the savage tried to wrest it free, Wiglaf drove his sword through the attacker's ribs and out his back. He put a boot in the savage's chest and kicked him away, freeing his sword just in time to swing it in a deadly backhanded arc and take the head from a skull-man about to drive his spear into a fallen Scylding.

Beowulf and five of his comrades were still standing, outnumbered at least double. Unable to swing his sword, Beowulf drove it into the rocky ground beside him and drew his poniard, holding its pommel against his hip. A pair of the screeching savages rushed at him from two sides. He twisted his torso to skewer one with his blade then grabbed a handful of the other's hair and kicked his feet from under him. As the savage fell, Beowulf spun him to drag his throat along the edge of the embedded sword.

Three of the attackers seized the stunned Ragnar and tried to pull him to the ground where they could stab at him under his mail with their crude knives. Athelstead swung his axe and with one blow cut the nearest one's leg off at the knee. He spun with the momentum and brought it down between the shoulder and neck of a second , cleaving him to his breastbone. He was freeing the blade when one of the tribe swung his club and embedded its teeth in Athelstead's knee. He roared in pain and fell. His attacker was raising the club for another blow, when Beowulf's dagger burst through his throat.

Only four of the skull men were left, and at a shrill whistle, they turned as one and fled, disappearing into the brush.

Beowulf stood staring after them. He gave a Berserker's roar of triumph then turned to his men. Three lay dead, and four others bled from their wounds, as did he from a slash across his calf. He turned to Wiglaf and said, "Who lives among us?"

"Eight in all. Twice their number are dead."

The clearing was strewn with bodies and primitive weapons. Beowulf crouched beside one of the skull men and wiped at his face. The red pigment came off like blood in his palm.

"Beowulf," said Wiglaf, "Here are Ragnar's two right feet." Instead of shoes, the dead man wore sandals with wooden soles, carved to look like paws.

"They sought to disguise themselves as animals, or to frighten as monsters."

"Shall we pursue them, my lord?"

"They have found what waits for them here. Let the survivors take the tale of this battle to their tribe. They will not come again."

"And their dead?"

"They fought bravely, as did we. Leave them where they lie. This is no conquering army. Once we are gone, they will return for their dead to honor them in whatever way their gods may decree. To hold that away from them would turn forage into vendetta. Let them take their dead and go. "

Wiglaf hesitated, as if he wished to say more, but his eyes met his leader's and he turned away to see to his comrades. The party bound their wounds as best they could and carrying their own dead, trudged back to Heorot.

†††

Later in the day, Wiglaf sought out Beowulf and found him once again at the precipice, gazing into the cataract below.

"Friend Beowulf," he said. "Once again I interrupt your thoughts."

"Well that you have come, Wiglaf. These thoughts perplex me. Perhaps you can help me to make sense of them."

"What troubles you so?" Wiglaf said, although he already knew.

"You saw me in today's battle."

"Yes, my liege. You fought well."

"But without my sword. My arm could not lift it."

"How did you injure it?"

"I did not." Beowulf held it out before him and flexed his fist. The tendons stood out like cables under his skin. He stood and strode to a fallen tree, knelt beside it, and wrapped his hand around a limb. He grunted with the effort, but one-handed, ripped the limb from the trunk and threw it far enough for it to bounce over the edge and fall into the cataract.

He stood and held up his hand, palm forward. "Wrestle me, Wiglaf."

"My liege, I would not presume—"

"Indulge me."

Beowulf and Wiglaf stood foot to foot and clasped each other's right hands. At Beowulf's nod, Wiglaf's grip twisted and pushed against Beowulf and he felt his leader's hand giving way. Beowulf's teeth showed in a grimace of effort, but slowly, his grip lost ground to his comrade's. Released, his arm fell to his side.

"I have lost the strength in my sword arm, but I have not. I am strong in all but contention."

"Witchcraft."

Beowulf nodded in agreement. He recounted the visitation of the succubus. "I have been cursed, Wiglaf, perhaps because I killed the monster Grendel and his wretched hag of a mother."

"Or perhaps at the behest of someone who would see you fall."

"Every man has enemies, but not many who would trade soul for revenge."

"But some might trade soul for crown."

"Unferth."

Wiglaf nodded. "Hrothgar's nephew. He would be one. Disabled in battle, you would no longer be favored by Hrothgar as protector and champion. The wheel turns. The past falls before the present in all things."

"But to accuse one of Hrothgar's kin with no proof could be deadly in itself. Hrothgar has taken me as family, but no bond is stronger than one's own blood."

"And you would be seen as scheming to rid yourself of Unferth's opposition and push Hrothulf and Hrethric aside to take the crown when Hrothgar dies, a clever trap, indeed."

Beowulf's brow darkened. "I have never sought a crown. All I have ever asked is a good fight, sword on sword where I can look my enemy eye to eye and let the gods decide whether I am worthy of living. I have no mind for dealing with these daggers in the dark."

"But necessity falls upon you, and you must rise to meet it with the weapons you yet possess; courage, cleverness, and will."

Beowulf sighed. "You are a good friend, Wiglaf, and a true comrade. I regret that my woes have become your own."

"I would be no man if I saw you falling and did not hold out my arm to catch you. You are liege, friend and brother to me, and I give you my oath that if this game proves to be your undoing, it will prove to be Unferth's as well."

✝✝✝

That night the survivors sat at the place of honor, the right hand of Hrothgar. Welfen the blind bard sang a song of Heorot's glory as his fingers nimbly coaxed a tune from his many-stringed harp. As they ate and drank, Hrothulf rose, a horn of mead in his hand. "Let us drink to Beowulf," he said, "the fiercest of warriors and leaders of men. When we were attacked by the skull-men, he stood firm, and inspired us all. Today's battle deserves a song, Welfen; words to celebrate Athelstead and his axe, Wiglaf and his sword, and Beowulf fighting with shield, poniard, and even a sword thrust into the ground to destroy the enemy."

"Into the ground, you say?" The speaker was Gaalen, friend to Unferth and partner in his many schemes. "Mighty Beowulf, would you stab at the heart of the Earth Mother, giver of all things?"

Silence fell. All eyes in the hall turned to Beowulf. He looked up from his cup and his eyes met Gaalen's with a glare that made Gaalen regret his remark. He began to stand, but Wiglaf laid a hand on Beowulf's shoulder and stood instead to be heard by all ears.

"We fight to hold the gracious gifts the Earth Mother has given to our king; to allow them to be taken would be an ingratitude. Beowulf merely opened Her mouth that She might drink the blood of our foes, and drink She did. Near a score of the skull-men nourished Her this day. As the cut worm forgives the plow, so does the Earth Mother forgive the wounds of necessity. And when two of the savages attacked our liege at once, two blades proved better than one."

An approving roar at this riposte rose among the men at table, pounding their mugs and horns on the benches. The chant, "Beowulf! Beowulf!" echoed through the hall, and Gaalen, red-faced, turned away. At his seat at Horthgar's left hand, Unferth neither smiled nor frowned. He looked over the heads of the chanting warriors, to read his future in the smoke ascending to the ceiling.

Two nights hence, the Scyldings were gathered again in Heorot for a meal when the sound of their revelry was interrupted by the pounding of a mailed fist on the great two-leaved door. Hrothgar waved his hand at Boltan, the doorkeeper to open it. The warrior raised the bar and the iron-strapped door swung wide to a warrior clad in mail and helm. A broadsword hung at his belt.

"Enter Heorot as friend," Boltan warned, "or leave on your shield."

"Good King Hrothgar," said the guest in a bold voice. "I enter your mead hall with no malice toward you."

"Then enter, as friend, set aside your sword and take a seat at our table," Hrothgar answered, too consumed by the mead to understand the trickery in the visitor's words. "Be our guest."

"I thank you, good king." The visitor sat at the bench with Hrothgar's men and took his meal without speaking, listening instead to the tales and the songs of the bard. More than once, Beowulf caught the newcomer watching him with hooded eyes.

Finally, it came the visitor's turn to share a tale or song. "Come, my friend," said the King. "You have traveled from afar, and I have no doubt that you have a tale we have never heard. Please, tell us of your travels and adventures."

"Indeed, good Hrothgar. I have traveled many leagues from my home because the fame of your champion and his great victories over men and beasts and monsters has reached the ears of the Southland. I have come to stand face to face with this mighty warrior named Beowulf, for I am Breca, son of Beanstan."

Silence fell around the room. Unferth spoke up. "The same Breca of the much vaunted swimming contest? The one whom Beowulf defeated so roundly, and the one whom Beowulf saved with one hand as he pierced the hearts of the great sea monsters with his other?"

"I am the same Breca of the swimming match," the guest replied, "but I dispute your account. I am come to set the story aright so that it does not

"...for I am Breca, son of Beanstan."

chase my heirs down the road of the ages and mock my family's name."

"But we all have heard the story from the mouth of Beowulf himself," Unferth said, and made a sweeping gesture with his arm. "And there he sits, friend Breca, to tell it again."

"A tale laced with half-truth and boast."

Wiglaf leapt to his feet at the insult, hand on his sword, but Beowulf laid a hand on his arm. "Let him speak."

Breca strode before the king and said, "I have heard the tale that Beowulf tells from travelers who have had the good fortune to enjoy your hospitality, good King. It is a tale that casts me as the lesser of men, as a coward, and as being indebted for my life to him. That is not so."

"Let the King hear your story, friend Breca," said Unferth, "that he may decide what is true."

"This is outrage!" snarled Wiglaf.

A troubled frown crossed Hrothgar's brow. "Breca, I have embraced Beowulf as my own son, and his deeds before our faces have proved his worth and prowess. He has slain the hell-fiend Grendel, the mother of monsters, and her brood, and to this day he serves as my protector."

"The world of men and gods knows that you, King Hrothgar, are the most just among kings," said Breca. "Please do not deny me the right, as your guest, to clear my name that it might not shame those who follow after me."

"If he lives to have heirs," Athelstead hissed.

"What say you, my King?" Unferth said. "Shall you afford your guest the hearing that hospitality demands?"

Hrothgar cast his eyes to Beowulf and saw no fear in them. "Truth will out. Tell your story, Breca."

"You have heard," Breca said, "of the great swimming match between Beowulf and me; how we breasted the waves for seven days and nights. I admit my folly in accepting so deadly a challenge, but I was loath to disgrace my father's house with cowardice, so I fell in with the reckless son of Ecgtheow, and we set out into the sea.

"But it was I, not he, who won that contest." Breca pointed an accusing finger at Beowulf. "He tells that on the fifth night, I lost heart and left him alone to do battle with the creatures of the sea. In truth, I stayed the course full seven and unlike he, I returned to my own shore at my own hand, while he, unable to command his own course, was borne by the waves to the shore of the Finns. I bested him in strength and prowess, yet he boasts to this day that I did not."

"What say you, Beowulf?" Hrothgar said.

Beowulf stood. "Lies." A murmur rose around the room. "It was not I, but Unferth here who recalled the tale of our contest, and the tale he told sounds like your telling. I did naught but set Unferth straight. I need boast of nothing. My deeds of today eclipse the past. Tell the story as you may, it does not change the truth."

"You also tell that I have never proved myself in combat," Breca said, "and I come to set that aright as well. Since last we met, many have I cleft, soul from bone, by the edge of my sword. I say 'truth,' you say 'lies.' Let the gods decide." He pointed his finger at the thane. "I challenge you, Beowulf, son of Ecgtheow, in defense of my name. Let the gods decide."

"You challenge this man?" Hrothgar said, incredulous, pointing to Beowulf.

"What could be more just than to let the gods choose the victor?" Unferth said. "That is his right, my King, as a guest under your roof."

Hrothgar gave Unferth a baleful look then nodded sadly. "That is so." He turned to Beowulf. "What say you, my fellow Scylding?"

Beowulf stood, faced Breca, and spoke with cold menace. "I accept the challenge, my King."

"My liege, you…" Wiglaf broke in, but Beowulf raised a hand to silence him.

"Very well," said Hrothgar. "A challenge has been offered and accepted. Three days hence, the matter will be settled by combat."

"Three days, my Lord?" said Unferth. "Why let this matter fester? Why not settle it now and be done with it?"

The King's stare silenced Unferth. "If a man is to put his life in the hands of the gods, it is meet to allow him the time to petition their favor. You seem eager to see blood spilled. If you are in such a rush to end this, take up a sword and fight Breca yourself here and now on behalf of your fellow Scylding." Unferth was silent. "I thought not." Hrothgar turned to Breca. "Three days hence, return to Heorot, and at the sun's rise your challenge will be satisfied. Now, Breca, take your leave."

Breca bowed. "I thank you, King Hrothgar." He cast one final look at Beowulf and strode out of the hall, as the great door closed behind him. Beowulf felt no fear, for fear was unknown to him, but he sensed in Breca's words, his manner, and his gaze, no anger, no hatred, only purpose.

†††

Wiglaf hissed, "It cannot be mere coincidence that no sooner does your sword arm falter than Breca appears. This is Unferth's doing." The pair stood away from the mead hall where none could hear their words.

"It seems so," Beowulf replied, staring into the darkness.

"Unferth has spun a clever net. If you lose to Breca, you are discredited in the eyes of King and clan. You could never ascend to rule, even if you wanted the crown. And young Hrethric, to whom you have pledged your support would suffer with your fall from grace. Hrothulf would ascend to the throne, and bend his ear to Unferth's counsel. Had you refused the challenge, the result would be little different."

Beowulf was silent for a moment. "What you say is true. But you have not said what might happen should I win. Is my fate set in stone?"

"My lord, I did not intend to — "

Beowulf dismissed the comment with a wave of his hand. "Hrothgar's sight has dimmed with age, and yet he sees the schemes of men. He suspects a trick, else he would have had me draw sword the moment the challenge was made. His word has granted me the time to prepare for this contest. By the laws of the clan, since Breca has made the challenge, it is my privilege to choose the weapons. I must choose wisely what I may wield to good advantage."

"Friend Beowulf," Wiglaf said, "Would that I could fight this Breca in your stead."

"There are but two ways a man becomes immortal in this life, Wiglaf; through his sons and their sons' sons, and by the songs of his people. I have no heirs and may not live to sire one. I will not have the bards sing of my name and cowardice in the same breath through the ages to come.

"I must meet this challenge myself. To do less would sully my name as surely as would defeat. One of us, I or Breca, must kill the other, or the lie and the truth will war with each other for all days. I have always fought on the attack, counting on strength and boldness to carry the day. Now, I must turn my mind to thoughts of evasion, defense, and guile. If I cannot be Tyr, I shall be Loki. It is not my way, but to win is to live. I will do what I must."

"Then what can I do?"

"You can trace this poison tree to its root; learn whether it is truly Unferth who set this plot in motion, and wherein lies the source of my enchantment."

Wiglaf nodded. "I shall, and I promise you this; should you fall to Breca's blade, Unferth will die before the next sun."

"Together, we may scotch this scheme before it succeeds. You pursue its birth, and I will pursue its death. My arm may be weak, but my guile for the fight is all the stronger. Sleep, if it comes this night, may bring wisdom. Let us seek it out."

✝✝✝

The next morning, Beowulf crossed two vales and came to the rude daub and wattle hut of Vortigern the ironmonger. Behind the hut stood a domed tent twice the size of his home, hides stretched over bent poles, where Vortigern's fire pit burned night and day.

The sun had barely risen, but the smith was already at his work, smoke from the burning charcoal slithering through the portal in the center of the dome into the chill morning air. The clang of Vortigern's hammer on iron pealed like the bell of doom, or the beat of a stern iron heart.

Beowulf opened the flap of the tent, and a rush of heat like dragon's breath blew through the opening. Though outside Beowulf could see his breath, inside the smith's tent was filled with the harsh heat of summer.

The scene from within was a page from Hell's own book. The walls of the tent glowed crimson then flared yellow as Vortigern pulled at the bellows rope to breathe air into the fire pit. The smith was a full span shorter than Beowulf, but by the thane's reckoning, two spans wider at the shoulder. Stripped to the waist, Vortigern's torso gleamed with sweat. Myriad small spark scars dotted his skin, and cruel muscles writhed under those scars like living creatures when he swung his hammer.

"I mean no disrespect, my lord," Vortigern said without looking at the warrior, "but if I do not strike when the heat is white, my labor will be in vain."

"Do what you must, Vortigern. I am here at your sufferance, not you at mine."

Vortigern pulled a bar of white hot iron from the forge. The metal bubbled and spat sparks. He laid it across his anvil and swung his hammer full, bending the iron like a forearm at the elbow back onto itself and pounded the doubled iron into a single thick mass. This he flattened out and shaped with his hammer, sparks following the anvil's clang like glittering bees as the steel cooled from white to yellow, to red; then he plunged the emerging blade into the edge of the coals, away from the fire's heart.

"You make the weapons of war, and yet you also forge the hinges that swing every door wide. Your craft is its own kind of magic," Beowulf said.

Vortigern smiled proudly. "It brings the Elements; Fire, Air, Earth, and Water into concert, my lord; the fire of the forge, the breath of the bellows, iron of the earth, and," he shook his head to the side, and droplets of sweat spattered, hissing, into the fire pit, "the sweat of a good man's brow."

"You know who I am," Beowulf said, making a statement of the question.

Vortigern nodded. "You are Beowulf, slayer of Grendel and favored of King Hrothgar. How may I serve you, my lord?"

"I have been challenged. You have heard of this?"

"Word flies like scattered starlings. There is none in Hrothgar's kingdom who by now does not know the story. Do you need a fine sword for this battle, mighty Beowulf, perhaps an axe of good clean iron?"

Beowulf smiled grimly. "I have something different in mind, something to test your skill and your speed, for the time is short."

"To aid the thane who delivered us all from the monster Grendel's wrath, no task is too great."

Beowulf picked up a piece of slate and a bit of soapstone. "As I slept last night, the gods favored me with a vision." He began sketching a design. "This is what I want you to build."

✝✝✝

Wiglaf too was busy. He followed the crooked path from the mead hall into the forest to the hut of the old blind bard Welfen. As the path wound like a serpent through trees, rocks and brambles, Wiglaf marveled that the old man could find his way home at all.

He soon came to a thatched hut in a small clearing and called out, "Welfen! You have a visitor."

From within the hut came a voice whose strength and clarity belied the balladeer's age. "It is young Wiglaf, is it not?"

"Not so young as I once was, but your ear is as sharp as your wit."

The flap over the doorway swung aside, and Welfen stepped out into the chill morning air. "To one who has lived as many winters as I, all men are young." Welfen, once tall and strapping, now stood crooked, wisps of white hair framing a wizened face and black, unseeing eyes. "Please, enter and share my fire." He stepped aside, holding the flap open, and Wiglaf entered the hut.

Inside, Wiglaf saw a rough wooden table and stool, a pallet covered with shaggy animal skins, and a dry stone hearth built like a kiln. Welfen's many-stringed harp hung from a leather thong beside the hearth. "I have but one stool; you may use it."

"Let us sit together, on the ground, my friend," Wiglaf said, "Neither higher than the other."

Welfen laughed, a deep melodic sound. "So, good Wiglaf, what brings you to the hearth of an old man on this good day?"

"I would hear a song, my friend." Wiglaf pressed a coin into the old man's palm.

"And what shall it be?" His smile showed his last three teeth. "A song of glory in battle? A ballad of love or lust?"

"Your songs hold the history of Heorot, its people, and its forebears. I would have you sing a song of Magda the sorceress."

Welfen's smile faded. "That is a song I do not sing often, but you are the second to ask for it in a fortnight."

"And the first?"

Welfen hesitated. Wiglaf pressed another coin into the bard's hand. The old man shook his white locks. "It is not gold that is precious to me, Wiglaf, but what few days that remain. My sons were killed in battle many years hence, and I have no heir to pass on the songs of our tribe. I must train another to take my place before I die, or the past of our people will be lost forever."

"I give you my word, Welfen, that none shall raise a hand to you. The life of Beowulf lies in your palm. But so that you do not speak the name and be blamed for it, I will say it for you. If you do not deny it, I will know that it is he. Unferth."

Welfen remained silent.

"Now, good Welfen, the song."

The bard rose and took his harp from its peg. He sat on the stool by the table as Wiglaf sat at his feet. The spiny fingers began to pluck notes from the strings, slowly, warily at first, then with confidence as they wove a haunting melody that spirited Wiglaf away from the world of now into the world of then.

†††

For the next two days, life went on in Hrothgar's kingdom, but below the surface of that life lay an edge of anticipation and of uneasiness. Word of Breca's challenge spread among all with ears, as did word that Beowulf had disappeared. Wiglaf too was absent, fueling rumors that the slayer of

Grendel, their champion and protector had fled. As the appointed time drew near, Heorot's people held their breath as one to see whether Beowulf would return to defend his honor.

The night before Breca's return, Heorot's warriors were gathered in the great hall at table when Unferth rose at Hrothgar's left hand. "Tomorrow is the appointed day for Beowulf to meet his challenge, yet I do not see his face nor his sword at this feast. Where might he be?" Unferth turned his head pointedly to scan the room from end to end. "Has he left us on the eve of his vindication? And has his faithful companion Wiglaf fled as well?"

Athelstead rose and strode across the room to stand before Unferth. Before anyone could speak or move, Beowulf's comrade drew his dagger. Holding it thumb over pommel, he raised his hand over his head and drove its point deep into the thick wood of the table.

"Before you again speak ill of my brother-in-arms, Unferth, you had best draw that blade from the table to defend your slanderous tongue."

Sensing his peril, Unferth wrapped his grip around the thong-wrapped handle and tugged at the dagger, but he could not budge it from its wooden sheath. Both teeth and knuckles showed white with effort, but Unferth could not wrest the blade from the table. His eyes widened as Athelstead leaned over the table and grabbed a handful of his hair and pulled his face toward the dagger's edge.

Gaalen and others of Unferth's company leapt to their feet, reaching for their swords but froze when Athelstead pulled Unferth's throat against the blade. "You mocked bold Beowulf for putting his sword in the earth, Gaalen. Let me prove the method's merit." Athelstead brought his face close to Unferth's and hissed, "Now, Unferth, I challenge you. Speak your mind."

Unferth was paralyzed with fear. His breath came in ragged gasps. His eyes rolled, imploring, to the King, but the King neither spoke nor raised a hand.

Athelstead turned to Hrothgar. "Good King, what is your will?"

Hrothgar raised a hand. "Unferth, a challenge has been given. Do you accept or do you refuse?"

Unferth gasped. "I — I refuse, my King."

"The lesson is learned." Then to Athelstead, "Release him."

He loosed his grip and Unferth reeled backward onto the bench. Athelstead easily plucked the dagger from the wood, twirled it in his fingers, and before he slid it home in his belt, cast his gaze across the room

Athelstead pulled his face toward the dagger's edge.

at Gaalen and his friends. "It is a fool who counts the harvest before the reaper comes, and a greater fool who gives that counting voice. When the time comes, Beowulf will acquit himself before all eyes." He glared at Unferth. "I spared your blood only so that you might live to see it."

Athelstead strode out of the great hall, and his companions rose and followed him, closing the great iron-bound door behind them.

†††

Wiglaf hacked his way through the vines and brambles of Deep Forest. Welfen's song was rich with image, but woefully short on detail. Two days he spent searching for the fabled bog that the crone Magda called her home. At night he lay awake, eyes wide and ears cast for peril, as Deep Forest came alive in the darkness. Welfen's song prepared him for the terrors he would face, but barely. The sun was about to rise on the day of Breca's return when he found the bog ringed by twisted trees and stunted undergrowth, lank grey weeds and sickly yellow moss.

He came alone to the wretched place, wishing to help his friend yet not wishing to jeopardize others of their company. Swords out, they would stand as one against any human foe, but Wiglaf was loath to put his comrades under the evil eye of sorcery, where one could lose soul as well as life.

The absence of birdsong gave him a first impression that men lurked about in the surrounding wood, but reason told him that no man would come to this forsaken place without good cause. Its very aura warned away even the most curious. No, whatever stalked these fens was not human.

Wiglaf peered into the dank water of the bog and saw nothing below its surface. He doffed his helm but kept his mail and sword as he ventured into the dun colored pool. Feeling with the tip of his blade, he plumbed the bottom for the entrance to Magda's cave that Welfen's song described. At the sound of a splash behind him, Wiglaf spun, swinging his sword in an arc and taking the head from a fanged serpent. The snake's thick body writhed, churning the water and turning it red with its vile blood.

The thane moved more quickly, certain that the blood and disturbance would alert others of the serpent's kind. He probed the stones and roots at the shallow bog's bottom until suddenly his blade found emptiness. Here then was the storied portal where he would gain entrance to the witch's den. "Gods protect me," said Wiglaf as he drew in a great breath and plunged feet first into the hole.

The opening sloped downward for a time then up again, where Wiglaf broke the surface and gulped in air that was less than wholesome. The dank smell of the cave was worsened by the odor of burning resin from pine splints stuck in the walls and something else that he recognized as burning flesh. The portal opened onto a small chamber, scarcely tall enough for him to stand. Dread held his feet fast to the rough stone floor for a time, but Wiglaf screwed up his courage and ventured deeper into the cave. As he passed side tunnels, he heard rustling, chittering, and now and then a gurgling chuckle from whatever hid in the darkness.

Beyond a twist in the passage, he entered a high-ceilinged chamber brightly lit by living souls with their heads afire, bound to stakes sunk into the floor. His heart recoiled in horror, but his face could betray no fear. Across the room on a dais sat a rude chair, throne-like with a tall back, and in it sat the cadaverous witch. Wiglaf could scarce bear to look upon the withered, bony horror that ages ago had been a beautiful young woman.

From behind her throne, a man-thing, blacker than black crept to crouch beside her. "We have a visitor," Magda rasped. "Gogalog, you did not tell me that I might prepare to greet him properly."

The thing gurgled, "Mistress, I…"

Magda flicked her wrist and a blue flame shot from the tip of her finger. It engulfed Gogalog's head, and the demon shrieked in pain, rolling on the rough floor in agony, but though the fire blazed brightly, Gogalog's skin was not burnt. As quickly as the flame burst forth, Magda extinguished it with a wave of her hand.

She regarded her visitor with a curious eye. He too had some magic, for she could not see into his head or his heart to divine his intentions. Whatever they may be, Magda said to herself, I will steal that magic from him and make my own all the more powerful. "Now my fine warrior," she said aloud, "what business have you with old Magda?"

"Mistress Magda, I am Wiglaf," he said. "I have heard tales of the great promise your affection offers, and I am come to woo you."

✝✝✝

Breca rode out of the morning mist astride a tall horse, sword at his side, armored in mail and plate. He rode through the open gates onto the hard-packed earth of the yard before Heorot's doors, dismounted, and stood unmoving, waiting to be recognized. Behind him, the sun rose red, tinting the fog that wound in tendrils around his armored feet.

The doors opened, and Heorot's men came out with King Hrothgar and his sons at the lead. The men filed into the foreyard and formed a semicircle with Breca at its center. "Welcome, Breca," said Hrothgar.

"Good King," said Breca, "I come to clear my name and the honor of my house. It is the break of day. Where is Beowulf? I do not see him among your warriors."

"Yes," Unferth sneered. "Where is Beowulf?"

A voice cut through the murmurs of the gathered clan like a well-swung axe. "Beowulf is here."

The crowd parted like the leaves of the great door of Heorot as the thane stepped into the yard. Beowulf strode forward. He wore no plate, only his mail, and neither sword nor poniard on his belt. He carried his war-dented helm under one great arm and a hide-bound bundle under the other.

Beowulf stood before Hrothgar and nodded his head in respectful greeting. "My King," he said. "I thank you for this day and for your wise judgment. As Breca has the right to challenge, by the rules of the clan, I have the right to choose the weapons."

"It is so. What weapons do you choose?"

Beowulf untied the rawhide thong about the bundle and unrolled it on the ground. Before all lay a pair of maces two cubits long, with thick knurled heads at either end. "I choose these."

Breca stared coldly at the maces. "What folly is this? Would you have us club at each other like savages instead of fighting sword to sword like true warriors?"

Hrothgar spoke. "Breca, you come to my home and challenge one of my thanes, indeed one of my sons. Would you challenge my word as well?" Around him, Breca heard the shing of many swords clearing their scabbards.

"No, King Hrothgar. I meant no offense. It shall be as you say." He picked up both of the maces, weighed each in a hand and made his choice. He threw the other scornfully at Beowulf's feet. "On this day, I Breca, shall straighten that which is crooked, and prove the truth to be my own."

Beowulf raised the other mace and threw Breca's words back at him. "Let the gods decide."

From the crowd, Unferth's eyes glittered eagerly. The poison tree he had planted was about to bear fruit.

Hrothgar clapped his hands and the assembled warriors closed in a circle around the hard-packed earth leaving no escape for either man. "Begin."

Beowulf seized the ends of his mace and twisted them against each other. With a click, the weapon separated into two halves, joined by a span of chain. "What trickery is this?" shouted Breca.

The circle of warriors murmured in confusion. Unferth shouted, "Foul!" and some of his companions took up the cry. Hrothgar raised his hand. "Silence!"

Beowulf stood, legs planted firm on the hard-packed soil, and gripped the ends of his split mace in either hand. "Your mace is the same as mine, Breca. Open it, or use it as it be."

"I need no trick to kill you, Scylding," Breca growled and rushed at Beowulf, holding the mace in both hands like the handle of an axe. He swung a blow that would have crushed the warrior's skull had it landed well. But Beowulf dodged the strike, and rolled to the side to spring to his feet behind Breca. He let go of one end of his mace and whipped his arm to pivot the other on its chain. The armored head struck Breca's plate at his shoulder with a dull clank and left its mark deep in the armor.

Breca reeled under the force of the blow. Unferth's eyes widened. "How can this be?" he said under his breath. Breca turned and swung his mace again, but the unarmored Beowulf was too nimble and ducked his head as the mace whistled over it. He whipped the chained mace around his back, took it in his other hand, and struck Breca just above his knee.

No sooner did Breca grunt in pain than Beowulf traded hands and spun the free end on its pivot to generate force and brought the armored end to his foe's helm, making Breca stagger sideways. Breca roared in anger and charged at Beowulf, driving him backward with a scything onslaught. One blow would have surely crushed the thane's head, but he caught Breca's mace with the chain on his own, stopping the blow just short of his face.

Breca twisted his arm and drove the end of his mace into Beowulf's chest, pounding his heart, knocking him backward, and taking his breath for a moment. Had he fallen, Breca would have killed him at that moment, but Beowulf held his footing and dodged to the side, chest heaving, as Breca swung another deadly two-handed blow at his head.

Beowulf twisted to the side and with a movement honed by days of practice with the deadly weapon, spun the mace's head on its tether. Had Breca not raised his mace in time, Beowulf would have smashed his opponent's face with the ferruled head.

Breca abandoned all finesse and swung his mace like the clubs of the skull-men. One blow caught Beowulf's shoulder and sent him reeling backward. Blood oozed from the wound, and at the sight of it, Breca's ardor flared. He roared and charged Beowulf, crashing plate on mail into the unarmored warrior.

"Yes, yes," whispered Unferth as Beowulf stumbled and fell to the side and Breca rose over him for the killing stroke.

†††

In the witch's cave, Magda smiled wickedly. "You would woo me, Wiglaf? You seem fit enough to sate the desires of an old woman." She left her throne and stepped toward him. "Let me kiss you, my fine young suitor, that I may test your ardor." She strode toward Wiglaf, arms out to embrace him, but before she could touch him and put him under her spell, Wiglaf thrust his hand into his jerkin. A glittering chain flashed in the light of the human torches and looped over Magda's head. Hanging from the chain of silver was the cross of the Celts, runes stamped in the circle that surrounded its jointure that he had taken years before as spoil.

Magda shrieked as flames burst from the rags over her breast. Her clawed hands grabbed at the cross and painful sparks flew wherever she touched it. "Gogalog! Take this thing from me!"

But Gogalog did not obey. His blackness faded with Magda's power, and the ancient man who stood before Wiglaf crumbled into grey dust. Magda had sunk to the floor of the cave, a mere pile of bones. The witch's eyes glowed red with hatred, but their fire slowly waned until their last spark died, and with it, her magic.

From the dark tunnels, creatures with no name slithered and scuttled to avenge their mistress. Wiglaf drew his sword and hacked at the monsters that surrounded him on every hand. He would have fallen to their fangs, but for the voided spell that had held the underground warren safe. Wiglaf heard the creak and groan of great slabs of stone as they shifted and separated, and knew that destruction of the witch's den was at hand.

Stone separated overhead with a great crack, and the dank water of the bog cascaded into the cave. With it came the light of day that drove the creatures back into the darkness. Wiglaf swam for his life and broke the surface, gasping for air. He climbed onto the weed-choked bank and fell headlong, careless to his own peril, praying to the gods that he had broken Magda's spell in time.

†††

"Now," said Breca, "shall I avenge my honor." He swung the mace full force at Beowulf's head.

The thane felt a tingle like fire in his sword arm. He thrust his hand forward and caught Breca's mace in his grasp, stopping the blow. The pair struggled for the weapon, but Beowulf prevailed. With a twist of his arm, he wrested the mace from Breca's hand and sprang to his feet. The Scyldings roared approval at this turn of the battle. Beowulf raised the mace over his head and was about to crush Breca's skull with it when he saw the dazed look on Breca's face.

"Beowulf?" Breca said, blinking. "Is it truly you? What place is this?" And Beowulf realized that Breca had been enchanted as much as he.

Beowulf threw the mace from either hand to the ground. "My King," he shouted over the roar of the assembled thanes, "This man has been enchanted, as have I to draw us into this fight. I ask that you void Breca's challenge and show him your mercy."

Hrothgar raised his hand for silence. "Is this so, Breca?"

"My lord, I do not know. I am in this place without knowing how I came or why."

"Ask Unferth," Beowulf said. "I believe he can answer."

All eyes in the throng searched for Unferth, but Unferth was nowhere to be seen.

✝✝✝

That evening, Beowulf and Wiglaf sat once again at the edge of the precipice. Wiglaf had just recounted the story of the undoing of Magda and the destruction of the witch's cave.

"Unferth has disappeared," said Wiglaf. "I do not think he will show his face anywhere your name is known."

"None can say that the gods do not play tricks with the lives of men," Beowulf said, "yet our outcomes often lie in our own hands. Had I not fought Breca with the chain mace I saw in my dream, a weapon that delivered force without might, he would surely have killed me. One thing you have not told me, Wiglaf. How did you know that the Talisman of the Celts would destroy the witch?"

Wiglaf did not answer for a time. "Truth be told, my friend, I did not know. I gambled with your life and mine and won."

Beowulf cast his eyes over the precipice into the gathering shadows below, heard the rush of the wild river far below.

"This time."

THE END

We All Know Beowulf

Few people in the English-speaking world, educated in the public or private schools have not encountered the name Beowulf, even if only accompanied by an under-the-breath curse of an older sibling. The oldest epic in the English language, Beowulf has entertained, inspired, and (if you tried to read it in the original Old English) exasperated millions. Beowulf, however, did not exasperate Robert E. Howard, who employed him as one of the models for Conan the Barbarian, and who honored him with the poem, "And Beowulf Rides Again," which I had the privilege of publishing for its first time in my fanzine *The Spoor Anthology* in 1974.

As a ten-year-old, and as an adult teaching English Literature and Mythology all those years, I often wondered what Beowulf did in the intervening years between the saving of Hrothgar's kingdom and his fatal battle with the dragon as an aged king. When Ron Fortier told me he was developing a pulp mythology collection, I saw my opportunity to fill in a few of the gaps. I had a great time writing "The Schemes of Unferth." I hope you have as much fun with it as I did.

†††

FRED ADAMS JR. is a retired Penn State University English Professor who spends his days writing pulp fiction and his nights working as a singer-songwriter. His novel Dead Man's Melody has been nominated as Pulp Novel of the Year in this year's Pulp Factory Awards. Airship 27 Productions has published six of his novels since 2014 and has five more waiting in the wings. His titles include: *Hitwolf* 1 and 2, *Six Gun Terrors* vol. 1 and vol. 2, *C.O. Jones: Mobsters and Monsters*. He also contributes to Airship 27's anthologies. His original Sherlock Holmes anthology *The Affair of the Chronic Argonaut* is forthcoming from Pro Se Press. He lives in Mount Pleasant, Pennsylvania and describes himself as living "in perpetual terror of boredom."

Procrustes

BY
FRED ADAMS, JR.

A beard hung gold, though truly white by the blaze
Of a sizzling greenwood fire in the robber's cave.
His hands glowed red as he stirred the embers hot.
Yet hotter still as the fresh-cut faggots dripped
Their sap to hiss among the pulsing coals.

"So thus shall I roast the green and supple bones
Of Aegus' bastard son, and bitter joy
Shall be my recompense as his marrow drips
And dances in my private pit of hell.
Haephestus! Hear my words! You cannot turn
Your ear from my entreaty; you have lost
A son as fine as mine – young Periphrates,
To this spawn of Athens' cunning king."

The robber rose, and in his fists he clutched
A sickle and a mallet of pure iron.
Gold and crimson dancers flicked across
The hammer's polished face. The sickle's edge
Flashed a brighter shade.
                                "Haephestus! You
Among Olympus' deities are lord
Of iron. I pray you sanctify these things,
That they might serve as sacred implements.
And this—"
                He whirled to face a bed of iron
Whose red was not the hue of flame
                                                "Shall be
The altar of my sacrifice. Hermes!
To you is given patronage of thieves.
Grant me guile that I may now avenge
The lives of two, children of us both:

151

Yes, Sciron of the cliffs and Sinis were
Your servants in the robber's trade, but they
Were felled by one whose brashness knows no bound.
He murdered each with no remorse because
They would have plied their trade on him, and each
Was slaughtered by his own device, the gifts
Of your own hand to earn their bread. I beg
That you will grant me like for like, my due,
The justice that I crave. I would make
Him suffer death a second time if Dis
Would grant reprieve from hell's stern gate. I beg
Of you, for I truly crave his blood,
Deliver him to me – give me Theseus!

No more did echoes die in the giant's den
Than a footstep sounded at the cavern's mouth,
And Polypemon turned to meet a man
Whose face he had never seen, but whose name
Was scored forever in his heart and brain.
Within himself, a cold voice spoke that none
But gods could hear:
                        "So this is the assassin?
Killer of my sons, this stripling whelp?
How vain he is to flaunt the stolen club
Of Periphrates, virgin iron fire-forged
In Aetna's molten heat. And shameless too,
He wears naught but his sword and sandals, those
That Aegus left behind, his legacy,
Like one who leaves a brothel in such haste
As to avoid discovery. Damn him
For the arrogance that bade him shave his head
Before but nor behind; a brazen boast
That none could ever seize him from the rear
For he would never flee from battle's heat.
That fear makes feet too swift would be nearer truth.
To shed his blood will be exquisite pleasure."

Polypemon smiled. "And who are you,
Young friend?"

The firelight tinted Theseus' skin
A shade of richer bronze so that he looked
To be a statue cast by gods themselves.

"A traveler to Athens asking rest
And food in the name of Zeus. And who are you?"

"A host who never turns away the weary
Or the hungry. Come inside."
                                    They sat
Beside the fire. In Theseus' eye, his host
Saw dancing flames that glittered from within.
The spark of madness blazing bright outshone
The cooking fire and cast its own dire shade
Upon the walls. They ate their meal in silence,
But with the wine, Theseus spoke:

                                    "Tell me,
my host, your thoughts on human destiny."

"The gods rule human lives, but ever they
Must yield before the brass-bound law the Fates
Prescribe for all existence. None escapes
Their stern dominion. Are there other thoughts?"

"I say each man decides his lot himself,
That what he chooses, he will then become,
If courage, craft and skill are his to ply
To better his advantage. I say men
Alone are masters of their fates if they
Are not afraid to break the bonds that bind
Them to a stake of abject misery.
The tales of gods who plan Man's destiny
Are foolish lies allowing Him to blame
Another for his follies and his faults
While seeds of failure flourish in his bones,
A mere excuse for blunder. What is your
Reply to my conception?"
                                    "I can make

No argument to change your view, so all
I have to say is this: it surely must
Be Fate compelling you to reason thus,
The gods have foreordained your heresy."

"To me Fate is the greatest tyranny,
To force its will upon another's life.
I find such answers wearisome."

                                                "Then please,
Accept my hospitality and spend
This night here in my home."
                                        The words were slick.
They rolled from Polypemon's tongue with ease
So many times he played the cordial host
To later work his torture on his guests,
Giving up his bed that they might sleep.
Then with his iron tools he made them fit;
The short were hammered longer and the tall
Were amputated, earning him the name
"The Stretcher," feared by one and all, Procrustes.

The statue slept on the bed of iron, his breath
As steady as the distant sea-waves, yet
Procrustes crouched beyond the scarlet glow
Of the embers, tools in hand. He did not dare
Be anything but certain. Finally,
He rose and crept across the rocky floor
To stand beside the bed. His hammer poised,
A whispered prayer upon his lips.
                                        "Oh gods
Grant me that which is my due, that he,
The slayer of my sons shall suffer more
Than they did at this monster's vicious hand."

Procrustes would have struck, but as the last
Few words were spoken, Theseus' eyelid raised.
Procrustes halted, frozen by the gleam
That shone of death from Theseus' staring eye.

Procrustes lay upon the bed, his bones
Smashed like kindling for his evening fire,
Blood oozing from the stumps of severed limbs.
He turned his head to gaze at his tormentor,
Gleaming with exertion's sweat. He spoke:

"So, Theseus, are you satisfied, content
With the fame your mighty deeds will earn
To make you live beyond the call of death?"

"I have proved my point, Procrustes, I
Have mastered Fate and bent it to my will.
I have destroyed the tyrants of the earth
By trapping all in snares of their own making,
Made myself a man of fame as I
Had sworn so many years ago, No god
Would dictate such a fate for a peasant's son."

Procrustes laughed.
                    "You have indeed destroyed
A tyranny, but in so doing, you
Have made another, greater still. When good
And evil coexist, too does a balance.
But when they walk one path, who can say
That one is not the other? Tell me, please,
Which of us is the greater tyrant now?
Do you believe no Fate controls your life?
For you I feel no less than deepest pity."

Theseus' eyes blazed angry. "Pity me?
You are a fool. At least I have a life
To live, and you have nothing."
                              "But I have
Some comfort in the credence that my fate
Has made me what I am, and I can die
At peace. Will you have such an easy death?
Or will your end elude you like a shadow
As you realize that no one else can bear

Your anguish at what you became, the same
As none can share your guilt. The gods have made
An answer to my prayers! My deathbed curse
Will haunt you all your days. I have my vengeance!

Theseus' face flushed deeper than the embers.
As he fled the cave, Procrustes' mocking laugh
Pursued him through the shadows of the moon.

BIRTH OF A LEGEND

In 1190, two years after wresting the crown from his father, Henry II, Richard the Lionhearted departed France for the Holy Lands and the Third Crusade. He left behind regents, Hugh, Bishop of Durham and his chancellor, William de Longchamp. But his younger brother, Prince John, lusted after the crown and saw Richard's absence as a golden opportunity to seize control. John began a program of heavy taxation that threatened to destroy the social-economic stability of England.

While the royals conspired against each other, it was the people of the land who suffered. Working under inhumane laws, they became no more than indentured slaves to the landed gentry. Amidst this age of turmoil and pain, there arose a man with the courage to challenge the aristocracy and fight for the weak and helpless. He was an outlaw named Robin of Loxley and how he became the champion of the people is a timeworn legend that has entertained readers young and old.

Now J.A. Watson brings his own vivid imagination to the saga, setting it against the backdrop of history but maintaining the iconic elements that have endeared the tale of Robin Hood to readers throughout the ages. With beautiful covers by fan-favorite artist Mike Manley and interior illustrations by Rob Davis, this is a fresh and rousing retelling of an old legend, imbuing it with a modern sensibility readers will applaud.

Airship 27 Productions is extremely proud to present –

Robin Hood

KING OF SHERWOOD · ARROW OF JUSTICE · FREEDOM'S OUTLAW · FORBIDDEN LEGEND

PULP FICTION FOR A NEW GENERATION

AVAILABILITY INFORMATION AT: WWW.AIRSHIP27HANGAR.COM

SET SAIL FOR ADVENTURE

The greatest seafaring adventurer of all time returns to the high seas, *Sinbad the Sailor!*

Born of countless legends and myths, this fearless rogue sets sail across the seven seas aboard his ship, the Blue Nymph, accompanied by an international crew of colorful, larger-than-life characters. Chief among these are the irascible Omar, a veteran seamen and trusted first mate, the blond Viking giant, Ralf Gunarson, the sophisticated archer from Gaul, Henri Delacrois and the mysterious, lovely and deadly female samurai, Tishimi Osara. All of them banded together to follow their famous captain on perilous new voyages across the world's oceans.

So pack up your you traveling bags, bid ado to your loved ones and get ready to sail with the tide as Sinbad El Ari takes the tiller and the Blue Nymph sets sails once more; its destination worlds of wonder, mystery and high adventure.